**Quinn coul...
for being i...
town, an...
Kerstin...
a picture she made as a dam...
in distress.**

He certainly was no knight in shining armour, and
he'd do well to hammer that into his head.
Damsels needed men of virtue and honour, not
burned-out lawmen with revenge on their minds.

He could not—he would not—give in to his urge
to soften his stance.

He had a job to do.

Dear Reader

Welcome to our sizzling August line-up from Desire™ designed to make your summer go with a swing! Our **Man of the Month** from Mary Lynn Baxter is gorgeous Porter Wyman. As a tycoon he can handle anything, but as a single dad he's in trouble! And another hero faces fatherhood in the second **Bachelor Battalion** book. Only this new dad, Captain Jeff Ryan, finds a baby on his doorstep!

Anne Marie Winston is back this month with a sizzlingly sexy story. Ronan Sullivan and Deirdre Patten denied their passion for each other years ago— but now they're sharing a house… Watch out for the final part of Anne Marie's trilogy in September! And Emily Stockton is trying—but failing—to resist Zach Durham and his two charming kids, in the latest novel from another sensuous writer Sara Orwig.

Finally, Eileen Wilks's hero finds himself both lover and protector to his female boss. And Pamela Ingrahm brings us an undercover cop falling hard and fast for his suspect's twin sister!

Enjoy them all!

The Editors

The Texas Ranger and the Tempting Twin

PAMELA INGRAHM

SILHOUETTE

DESIRE

DID YOU PURCHASE THIS BOOK WITHOUT A COVER?
If you did, you should be aware it is **stolen property** as it was reported
unsold and destroyed by a retailer. Neither the author nor the publisher
has received any payment for this book.

*All the characters in this book have no existence outside the imagination
of the author, and have no relation whatsoever to anyone bearing the
same name or names. They are not even distantly inspired by any
individual known or unknown to the author, and all the incidents are
pure invention.*

*All Rights Reserved including the right of reproduction in whole or in
part in any form. This edition is published by arrangement with
Harlequin Enterprises II B.V. The text of this publication or any part
thereof may not be reproduced or transmitted in any form or by any
means, electronic or mechanical, including photocopying, recording,
storage in an information retrieval system, or otherwise, without
the written permission of the publisher.*

*This book is sold subject to the condition that it shall not, by way of trade
or otherwise, be lent, resold, hired out or otherwise circulated without the
prior consent of the publisher in any form of binding or cover other than
that in which it is published and without a similar condition including this
condition being imposed on the subsequent purchaser.*

*Silhouette, Silhouette Desire and Colophon
are registered trademarks of Harlequin Books S.A.,
used under licence.*

*First published in Great Britain 1999
Silhouette Books, Eton House, 18-24 Paradise Road,
Richmond, Surrey TW9 1SR*

© Paula D'Etcheverry 1998

ISBN 0 373 76170 8

22-9908

*Printed and bound in Spain
by Litografia Rosés S.A., Barcelona*

PAMELA INGRAHM

lives in Austin, Texas, with the man of her dreams and their two children. She's added one dog to the mix, who thinks the human race was put here to love her, and Pamela swears she's not doing anything to foster that notion. She also tells all who will listen how wonderful it is to live your dream.

Other novels by Pamela Ingrahm

Silhouette Desire®

Cowboy Homecoming
The Bride Wore Tie-Dye
Wedding Planner Tames Rancher!

To Rhonda—confidante, compulsive-shopping pal
and best friend.
You are more dear to me than you'll ever know.

Special thanks to Sergeant L.R. 'Rocky' Wardlow,
Texas Ranger, for his time and invaluable information,
not only to me personally, but to the Austin Chapter of
Romance Writers of America.

One

The sign at the edge of the city read Welcome To Hell.

And it was about to break loose.

Quinn O'Byrne shielded his eyes against a spray of glass, shaking his head at the group of wanna-bes who'd picked the wrong bar to play tough in. When one of the more aggressive regulars knocked the waitress into his table, Quinn took advantage of the opportunity.

Vaulting out of the booth, he hooked her around the waist and hauled her through the melee. The door slammed shut behind them, and the screen swung back on its stretched and rusted spring, eventually sputtering shut. The noise of the raging fight became muffled, and the night suddenly seemed quiet.

"You can let go now."

He carried her all the way to the dilapidated picnic table sitting under the heat-stressed leaves of an ancient oak. Leaning back against the edge of the battered table, he pulled her into the vee of his thighs and loosely locked his hands behind her. She didn't struggle against the intimate hold, allowing her stiff posture to send him an unmistakable message.

"But I'm trying to keep you safe," he said, opening his eyes wide in feigned innocence.

"A blind man could see what you're trying, Irish, but it won't work. Your blarney hasn't succeeded for the past couple of nights, and it won't now." Stepping backward, she broke his hold and sat on one side of the swaybacked table bearing testament to the number of knives the patrons of this establishment carried.

Quinn hid a grin as he shifted around on the tabletop and planted his booted feet on the bench beside her hips. He leaned back on his hands and watched the expressions chasing each other across the woman's beautiful face. She hadn't figured him out yet, which was fine with Quinn. He needed her to be intrigued.

As she said, he'd been around for the past couple of nights, so he had already cataloged the basics—she was about five-seven, probably a hundred and twenty pounds, had soft auburn hair and green eyes reflecting a soul-deep sadness despite her air of boredom. She was long and curvy and easy on the eyes. Especially his tired ones.

Kerstin Lundquist was completely out of place in the town of Hell, Texas. She was trying to play the part of a hardened waitress in a biker bar, but her modestly zipped leather vest and the cutoff shorts she constantly tugged down only made her appear to be playing dress-up. She walked around the bar as if she had a job to do—no sauntering, no flirting, no swaying of her hips. And maybe no one had told her that biker chicks didn't usually smell like a hint of sunshine and warm wildflowers under the cover of stale beer and cigarettes.

The incongruous picture was a sight better than anything he'd seen during his last assignment. Rustling was alive and well in Texas, a much more sophisticated, big-money game than that of a hundred years ago. Now thieves used semirigs and helicopters, but there was nothing like a good Texas-bred quarter horse for getting around the west side of the state. They'd been successful in busting the ring, but after a week in the saddle, a delicate face was a welcome change of scenery.

His vantage point provided him a wickedly delightful view of her cleavage, confirming she possessed the curves and the long legs to pull off the outfit, if not the confidence. The state of Texas paid him good money to be observant, and it was obvious to him that Kerstin didn't carry herself like someone comfortable in her attire.

"You can't blame a guy for trying," he finally said, giving her the smile he'd been told was his best come-on.

She arched a brow at him. "Then what can I blame you for?"

"For being a man smitten by a fire-haired beauty whose—"

"Please," she interrupted. "If my choices are clichés or butchered poetry, stick with the clichés."

Quinn was having way too much fun teasing her. He might be on a leave of absence, but he was still a Texas Ranger, and he did have a fair amount of honor. Then again, he'd left honor back at the office when he'd taken off his star with the full intention of killing the man who had taken his wife from him.

Every time he thought of Haley, a chorus of what-ifs attacked him. What if he'd taken better care of his marriage? What if his last words to her hadn't been in anger? What if he hadn't been out of town that night? Would the day ever come that Haley's face didn't flash before his eyes?

Her vacant stare was his last image of the woman who'd shared his life for five years, and most days he avoided sleep as long as possible to escape the guilt that haunted him. The only thing he lived for now was making Jackson Pepper pay for what he'd done. He had no hope for absolution, only that he might give Haley's spirit justice so she could rest.

"You've been trying for two days. Don't you know

when to give up?'' Kerstin asked, breaking into his reverie.

He forced the thoughts back into a corner of his mind and focused on Kerstin again. He might have believed she was as cool as her tart response indicated, if her hands weren't clenched together so tightly that her knuckles showed white.

He gave her a slow, easy grin. ''Let's just say I'm the persistent type.''

''Then you'd best be warned about what Daddy does to your… type.''

''Call me Quinn.''

She frowned. ''Pardon?''

''You called me Irish earlier. The guys call me that. I'd rather you called me Quinn.''

She thought for a moment. ''Not that I plan on calling you anything at all,'' she said grudgingly, ''but if I do, I like Quinn better.''

Quinn shifted his weight and settled a bit closer to her. ''So, what's a nice—''

''Girl like me doing in a place like this?'' she finished, rolling her eyes. ''Oh, brother. Just forget what I said about the clichés, okay?''

''It's a serious question,'' he protested. He gave her an obvious once-over. ''No tattoos—that sexy birthmark peeking over your waistband doesn't count—no body piercing, natural hair color, soft skin obviously lacking that special wind- and sun-dried effect.''

''What I'm doing here is not talking to you,'' she

said crisply as she swung her legs around the bench and headed toward the building.

Quinn jumped down and caught her arm. "It's not safe to go back in there yet." The sound of yet another shattering beer bottle proved his point.

She gave him a once-over that mimicked his of a moment ago. She probably didn't realize the faint blush still staining her cheeks spoiled her haughty air.

"It's safer than out here," she informed him, yanking her arm from his grasp.

Quinn smiled again. He couldn't help it. She was so blessed cute. He was sure he was supposed to be intimidated by her frosty attitude, but it wasn't having quite the effect she intended. He had to forcibly remind himself he was here to coerce information out of her. Hell, he'd seduce it out of her if he had to. Clearly, though, antagonizing her wasn't the smartest way to start.

He softened his expression. "Kerstin, I'm sorry. I've been picking on you. Come on." He nodded toward the picnic table. "Come talk to me some more."

She complied with obvious reluctance.

This time they both sat on the bench and rested against the tabletop.

"So, how long have you been working for Daddy?"

"About a month," she said absently, casting an impatient glance toward the door.

"That must be why I haven't seen you before. I haven't been down this way in a while."

She paused, then nodded noncommittally.

"You going to stay long?" he tried as another gambit.

"As long as necessary."

"For what?"

"To take care of what needs taken care of."

Quinn chuckled. "I love cryptic women."

Kerstin's lip twitched as she placed her elbows on the table and tilted her face to watch the sky. He was certain her ploy was supposed to make him feel ignored, but damn, her profile was gorgeous, lit by moonlight so bright the clouds cast faint shadows on the ground.

The woods behind Daddy's bar were typical of the Big Bend area. West Texas was starkly beautiful, cedar and sage tenaciously clung to the rocky soil of the land at the bottom of the Rocky Mountain chain— a backdrop that made Kerstin's natural grace stand out like a rose among thistles. Everything about her spoke of softness in a place known for sand and rock and blistering sun.

"Have you heard any word on your sister?" he asked in a voice matching the quiet.

Kerstin shot him a suspicious glance, and he held up his hands in mock-surrender. "Hey, I didn't mean anything personal. Word gets around, you know? There are no bigger gossips than a bunch of bikers on a road trip."

"Maybe," she admitted hesitantly.

Quinn brushed his hand across her shoulder for the

merest second. "I hear you're real worried about her."

She looked at him through narrowed eyes. "What would you know about it?"

"I caught up with Big Tex when I was in Del Rio and he said to tell you hello. He also said he hasn't heard anything about your sister yet."

Actually, Quinn wouldn't know Big Tex if the man came up and slugged him, but he did know that Daddy's best friend was now on his way to Austin, courtesy of the Val Verde County sheriff. Big Tex probably didn't have a message for anyone, except maybe a bail bondsman. Quinn was banking that Big Tex was one of the bikers helping to spread the word that Kerstin was looking for her sister, but he wasn't going to be much help from behind bars.

Quinn was also grateful he had a partner willing to pass along information he'd been ordered to stay away from. Randy was the best partner a man could ask for. Randy understood Quinn's need to be involved in the search for his wife's killer, and it was because of Randy's help that Quinn had found Kerstin, his biggest lead so far. Kerstin would lead to Meghan, and Meghan would lead to Pepper.

Quinn only hoped Kerstin's sister's monumentally stupid choice in boyfriends didn't end up getting her killed. The only way he could prevent that was to get Pepper's neck between his hands before the man did any more damage.

A barely perceptible easing to the cast of Kerstin's

shoulders nearly escaped his notice. It was exactly the sort of body language he could ill afford to miss.

"Big Tex, huh?" she asked.

"Yep."

"I thought he said he was headed home to Dallas. What was he doing in Del Rio?"

Quinn kept his face straight, and focused on the conversation. It was difficult, though, with the moon bathing her in a soft glow and the wind teasing him with her scent. Tendrils of her long, auburn hair tickled his face and neck, tempting him to bury his hands in the satiny softness.

His reaction to Kerstin confused and scared him. If he owed Haley nothing else, he owed her his loyalty until her spirit was at peace, and lusting after this woman cast doubt on his commitment. His mother would probably tell him nothing was haunting him except his own conscience, but his mother was an ocean away so he could hardly argue the point with her. For an Irish native, Mom was surprisingly non-superstitious.

Pulling out of his reverie, Quinn put his thoughts in order. "Big Tex is from Missouri," he said, answering her test. "I think he was headed for St. Louis."

"Oh, yeah," Kerstin said. He assumed he was supposed to believe her apparent confusion.

August was as hot as the name of the town deserved, but tonight a cool front promised rain. Silence serenaded them while the coming storm provided a descant of scuttling leaves. Kerstin sat forward as if preparing to stand again. "Sounds like things have calmed down in there."

Quinn stopped her with a sideways glance. "Why are you so afraid of me? All I've done is flirt with you."

He sat still as she appraised him from head to toe. He wasn't vain, but neither was he coy. He knew he was in great shape—not that he recommended a constant diet of bitter anger and pounding exercise—but it had made him lose the extra pounds he'd put on. Karate, which had once been a hobby, was now his passion, and hours of kata and sparring had replaced his paunch with rock-solid muscle. He'd inherited his father's dark Irish good looks and had every intention of using them for all they were worth. He had a man to kill, and he'd play the stud in a heartbeat if it meant getting the information he wanted.

His hair was long by Ranger standards. He wasn't used to feeling it brush the back of his neck, but his unkempt style was as much lack of concern as an attempt to appear a bit less clean-cut.

"I'm not scared of you," Kerstin eventually said, rising to his bait.

"So, you just don't like me?"

Kerstin surprised him by sighing and running her hands over her face. "It's not that I don't like you. It's been fun watching you act like a fool."

He caught the humor in her eyes and laughed. "Thanks."

"But...you're different. Sometimes you seem cold as ice when you're sitting in that booth, lost in thought. But then you smile, and you seem like an okay guy."

"Then flirt back with me."

She shook her head. "Too risky."

"For what?"

"For me. I've got things to do, and I can't get distracted."

"Things like finding your sister?"

She tensed again. "Yeah, something like that."

"So you're telling me you can't have any fun while you're waiting?"

Kerstin rolled her head forward, stretching her neck from side to side as though easing out the kinks. "I'm not exactly on vacation here."

Quinn waved his hand toward the sparse vegetation and the run-down building. "Are you casting aspersions on this little piece of paradise?"

Kerstin shook her head as she chuckled. "Of course not."

"So, if you like me—"

"I didn't say that—"

"Give me a chance to take your mind off your troubles. Let me take you to breakfast."

The social life of Hell had odd parameters. Bikers gathered at the bars along the strip, gradually leaving around two and three in the morning, at which point they congregated for breakfast at the many diners along the highway before heading to their respective beds.

"No, thanks. I'm going to help clean up and hit the hay. It's been a long weekend."

"Come on, Kerstin. You could use a full meal, and it's the least you owe me."

She jerked her head around at him. "Owe you?"

"Yeah, for saving your life."

"First of all, I didn't need saving, and second of all, I could have saved myself."

Quinn heaved a sigh, his shoulders slumping dejectedly. "Ungrateful and chicken. Just my luck."

"I don't do taunts well," she assured him dryly.

"Taunting? I wasn't taunting. I was merely coming to terms with the fact that you don't trust yourself to keep your hands off me through one tiny little breakfast."

Kerstin rolled her eyes again. "You flatter yourself, Irish. You're not *that* attractive."

"Really?" he asked softly, using his finger to wrap a strand of hair around her ear. "Then why is this—" he traced the delicate vein pulsing along her throat "—beating like mad?"

The back door burst open and Daddy appeared, hauling out two men by their shirts and lobbing them into the dirt. As their bodies hit with dull thuds, Daddy turned his snarling countenance upon Quinn.

"What the hell are you doing?"

Quinn lifted his hands, palms out. "Nothing. Just talking."

Daddy looked at Kerstin. She nodded.

"It's all right, Daddy. He grabbed me out of there when the glass started flying. I guess I didn't notice it quieting down."

Daddy studied Quinn for a long, assessing moment before deciding he didn't need to crack another skull and turned abruptly back into the bar.

Relieved that Daddy hadn't pursued the matter, Quinn followed Kerstin inside without argument. He could probably hold his own, even against Daddy's sheer mass, but the last thing he needed was to make the man angry.

The reduced crowd was significantly more subdued. Kerstin sighed, picking up a broom to sweep broken glass while Daddy worked on the bar. Quinn took a fresh beer to his seat. He shook the glass out of his leather coat, not a little surprised the expensive jacket was still there, and sat back to do what peace officers did most. He waited.

"Psst, beautiful. Over here," he whispered as Kerstin came near his table.

She glanced at him, annoyance marring her lovely features.

"Come to breakfast with me."

She shook her head.

"I promise not to stiff you with the tab."

Her lip twitched.

"I'll buy you a large orange juice."

The other side of her mouth jerked.

"I promise I won't tell Daddy you wanted to kiss me—"

"Shh!" she hissed, glancing back at the bar. Satisfied Daddy was occupied with his own cleaning, she stepped closer. "I did not. Don't even tease about that! Everyone knows Daddy acts like my father, and he'd kill you first and ask questions later if he thought you were being…inappropriate."

Quinn gave her a puzzled look. "You have got to tell me the story of how you hooked up with Daddy. Every time you say something, it makes me even more curious."

"Maybe I will, sometime."

"How about in thirty minutes? It's almost dead in here now."

"You aren't listening to me, are you?"

"Oh, Daddy," Quinn said, acting as if he were calling to the man who gave new meaning to the saying "ugly as sin and twice as mean." It didn't help that Daddy weighed as much as any two men in the bar, plus half of Kerstin added in for good measure.

"Stop that!" She cast another anxious look over her shoulder.

"You're worried about me," he said with an overdose of awe in his voice.

"I am not," she snapped, swiping her rag over the table in front of him. "I just don't want your broken carcass on my conscience."

"Come on, admit it. You care about me."

"Quinn—"

"Have breakfast with me."

"No."

"Then you leave me no choice." He slid out of the booth and took a step toward the bar. "I'll just have to ask Daddy's permission."

Her face paled a shade. And she didn't have much of a tan to lose. "All right, darn you."

"Darn me? Kerstin, Kerstin. Such foul language."

She glared at him. "Just go outside, and I'll meet you in a minute."

Quinn handed her a twenty to take care of his tab and generous tip. He denied the urge to check over his shoulder as he walked out, and would deny to his dying breath that he swaggered.

Kerstin dumped the last scoop of broken glass into the trash. She watched Quinn stop by the front pool table to talk to some of the regulars and wondered at the tightening in her stomach. What was wrong with her?

She'd learned not to cast everyone who rode Harleys as drug-dealing scum, but not once, before now, had she felt this gut-twisting attraction to any of the males she'd met since leaving Austin.

Her job as senior assistant at the brokerage firm of Henson & Henson had put her in contact with a number of handsome men. If she was going to be drawn to a man based on his physical appearance, she would certainly choose an up-and-coming investment broker over an itinerant biker. No matter how low she'd sunk in her efforts to find her sister, no matter how foul her language at times, or improper her demeanor, she was merely playing a part. Some day she would return to a world where her clothes covered more than the barest essentials.

She told herself the only reason she was going to breakfast with Quinn was to find out if he knew more from Big Tex about Meghan's whereabouts. She had already found the little things people said provided the best leads. Maybe Quinn had a bit of information and didn't even know it.

She leaned forward and flattened her hands on the bar as Daddy finished up. "You okay?" she asked casually.

A rare smile creased his tough, fleshy face. "Don't I look okay?"

She should have known better. "Well, it apparently didn't get too bad." Aside from myriad beer bottles, only one table had been a casualty. "Who started it?"

"Just a piece of scooter trash. I didn't know him."

Kerstin had quickly learned the names and faces of the regulars at Daddy's, and some of the more odd pairings. Fridays and Saturdays weren't much different here than at any other bar, except the clientele wore a lot of leather and drove motorcycles. Some folks were nice, some were surly, some were bright, some were dumber than dirt. She was still amazed that the majority of bikers who came to town held steady jobs. Then she'd found out how expensive it was to build and maintain Harleys, and she understood the necessity of "real" jobs even more. She'd made the mistake of comparing them to "normal people," and Daddy had nearly choked on his laughter.

She'd learned to put away her stereotypes and take his word for whom she should steer clear of. Daddy was doing his best to help her find Meghan, so Kerstin put up with his overprotectiveness. Funny, she hadn't felt the need for Daddy's intervention with a certain sexy Irishman....

She shivered at the reminder that Quinn was waiting outside.

"Do you know that guy—Quinn? Most of the guys call him Irish."

"I've seen him."

"He said he was a friend of Big Tex."

"I ain't Tex's mother."

"I was just wondering." She pushed away from the bar. "I'm going to have breakfast with him. If you hear me rattling into my trailer later, don't be worried."

Daddy gave her a grudging nod. He had built a little house just behind the bar and put a roof over the area between the two buildings where he normally kept his bikes. Right now, her trailer was sheltered there as though in a pull-through campsite, and her door faced the door of his house. She knew he kept his ears open at night, and she felt as safe as it was possible to feel, she supposed, knowing the man was guarding her property and her life.

She found Quinn outside, sitting sideways on his

Harley Electra Glide. The deep blue paint on the tank shone, even in the dim light cast by the bare bulbs surrounding the hand-painted sign announcing Daddy's Place. In her previous life, she'd never thought of motorcycles as beautiful, but she'd developed an appreciation for them since coming here. Fast-moving clouds obscured the once-bright moon and she was genuinely sorry she couldn't study the mystique-filled machine more closely.

Quinn was the picture of patience with his booted feet crossed at the ankles and his arms crossed over his chest. Kerstin envied the breeze playing with his hair. It was at the a-month-too-late-for-a-haircut length, and the opposite of the clean, crisp style worn by the men she was used to. Maybe that was part of what intrigued her. He was clean, if not clean-cut, and his eyes spoke of intelligence and mystery. He might bear little resemblance to the investment brokers she knew, but he wasn't like any of the other bikers she'd become familiar with, either. It teased the part of her that wanted things neat and orderly and in their logical place.

Her stomach somersaulted as he straightened from his relaxed position in one sleek move, and held out his hand.

She studied his long, outstretched fingers, warning herself to be careful before she placed her hand in his. He pulled her closer to the bike and mounted first.

"Here, put this on," he said, handing her his leather jacket.

With the wind picking up, it would have been foolish to refuse his offer. The ride would be too chilling in her sleeveless attire. As she slipped the jacket on, her senses were assaulted by the crisp, clean scent of aftershave. He was waiting, steadying the bike for her to climb on the jump seat behind him, but she had to take a second to close her eyes and calm her pulse.

As she put her feet on the kick bars, she hesitated again. Her thighs were already snugly pressed against Quinn's hips, and the sensation of denim scraping along her bare legs was doing a number on her heart rate. His pristine white T-shirt, tucked into his faded jeans, did little to hide his rock-hard torso, and the thought of wrapping her arms around him was the icing on an already intimidating cake. It was a little late, but she should have remembered that riding on the back of a motorcycle was an unavoidably intimate experience.

With a deep breath, she embraced him, attributing the warmth she felt to her high blood pressure, rather than Quinn's body heat lingering inside the leather.

She wondered if this was such a good idea after all....

Two

Good idea or not, Kerstin sipped her orange juice and waited for her omelette with surprising equanimity. The homey atmosphere of the pancake house was so starkly different from Daddy's, she had to remind herself to keep her guard up. Bright lights, cheery plants and ruffled curtains invited the customers to be comfortable and casual, and Kerstin didn't know if she'd be either ever again.

She had one goal, and one goal only: to find Meghan before she ended up dead. No matter how many times she reminded herself, Kerstin still found it difficult to believe this nightmare was real. There were times she expected to wake up and find herself at home, in her bedroom, trying to decide which of her stylish but reserved suits to wear to work. But day after day she found herself in her hastily purchased trailer, choosing between worn blue jeans and shorts, and T-shirts and leather vests.

Two months ago she'd never owned anything made out of leather. Now she had quite a collection.

Kerstin wished the unspoken communication she and Meghan had shared as children still worked. Whether or not it was telepathy by standard definition, they'd driven their mother crazy all through grade school with their seeming ability to know what the other was thinking. But now, as adults, all she seemed to send Meghan was disapproval. Having a flamboyant younger sister, even if only by thirty minutes, had been fun as teenagers. Kerstin hated to admit how much time, precious time, she'd wasted trying to make Meghan grow up.

She saw Meghan in a different light now, accepting her free spirit as unique instead of annoying. Kerstin tried to tell herself she'd been so hard on Meghan because of concern for her future, but she knew jealousy was also a reason. Meghan chose not to be restricted by other people's rules, and Kerstin envied her the freedom such choices provided. She'd always accused Meghan of running away from her problems, but the hard truth was, Kerstin was the real runaway.

This situation had forced Kerstin to see that she had run as fast as she could from anything that wasn't safe, comfortable and predictable. She'd been so busy maintaining her neat and ordinary world she hadn't seen how precious life really was.

Kerstin's hand tightened on her glass. She only hoped Meghan was going to get the chance to make her own decisions about her future, this time with her sister's love and support. Kerstin promised that if she could just find Meghan before that scum who'd swept her off her feet killed her, she'd never scold Meghan about being a female Peter Pan ever again.

Quinn returned to the table from washing his hands, forcing Kerstin to stop her mental wandering. She smiled tentatively as he sat down.

"You said you saw Big Tex in Del Rio, right?"

"Yeah, that's right."

"And you said he hadn't heard anything *yet*. Did he happen to say if he was waiting on information, or if he just didn't know anything at all?"

Kerstin hoped her voice didn't sound as desperate as she felt. Each new day, she forced herself to be patient to keep from going off half-cocked on the slightest rumor about Meghan. Daddy'd held her back, more than once, reminding her she needed more to go on than someone saying they *might* have seen a girl who looked like Meghan at such-and-such bar. Still, it was hard not to get her hopes up, even on dubious secondhand news.

Quinn frowned, as if trying to remember the week-or-two-old conversation. She wanted to scream at him to hurry, but managed to stay silent. She'd worked with enough men to know they didn't take prodding well.

He finally gave his head a little shake. "No, I don't recall him saying anything specific. I'm sorry."

He put his hand over hers, and Kerstin's stomach clenched. She knew he meant to be nice, but all she felt was trapped. The only way she'd known to survive these long weeks had been to shut down all her emotions except her need to find her sister. Now, in a matter of hours, a stranger—an utterly sexy stranger, true—had made her forget the worry and fear that had been her constant companions. His hand on hers, no matter how innocent, made her remember how scared she was, how lonely.

Why had he succeeded where the others who had flirted with her had not? Maybe it was because the other men had usually been three-quarters drunk, or maybe it was because a keen intelligence lurked behind this man's cobalt blue eyes. It could be because she never had time to flirt in her "real" life. She was too busy with work and with school. Nowadays, all she had was time—tension-filled, anxiety-ridden time. And something in this stranger called to her.

As carefully as she could, to avoid hurting his feelings, Kerstin pulled her hand back and tried to smile.

"Don't apologize. I appreciate whatever news I can get. I never know what little piece of gossip is going to be the key."

"What's her name?"

"My sister's? It's Meghan. I thought you knew."

"Big Tex didn't mention it." He shifted in his seat. "When was the last time you saw her?"

"About six weeks ago." She couldn't stop a flash of pain from creasing her brow. "We were arguing, as usual. It's all we ever do lately. I've finally realized our problems communicating stem from Meghan not acting the way I want her to." Kerstin's expression was self-deprecating. "Why can't we just accept people the way they are without trying to mold them in our own image?"

She saw something in his eyes, something saying he understood how much it hurt to be at odds with someone you love, but he quickly shuttered his expression and broke the momentary connection.

"Maybe, with this tension between you...maybe Meghan doesn't want you to find her. She's a big girl, isn't she?"

He said the words softly, tentatively. Kerstin had to work at controlling her angry response.

"You wouldn't understand," she said, a bit more curtly than she intended.

"Try me."

Kerstin felt her face grow taut. "My sister's in trouble, and she needs me. I can't stop looking for her. I just can't. It has to do with being a twin, and you wouldn't understand. Only another twin can."

"I may know more than you think. My wife was a twin."

"Your wife?"

He nodded.

Something shifted inside of her, and she didn't like the feeling at all. She didn't know what to name it; disappointment came close. Not exactly jealousy. The most disturbing of all was that she even cared whether the man was married or not.

"Your wife doesn't mind you going off on road trips by yourself?"

Okay, so maybe she was a little jealous. And a little mad at him for acting like a man and running off with his buddies instead of being with his wife.

"My wife is dead."

"Oh," she said softly. "I'm…I'm so sorry."

Compassion colored her voice, but she still felt like an idiot.

An ache darkened his eyes. He hid his reaction quickly, but it was enough to reach across the table and grab her by the heart. His expression became closed in an instant, his face a harsh, unreadable mask.

"Haley had a twin brother. They were very close."

Kerstin sat frozen in place as her nightmares attacked her, released from the pit she tried to keep them contained in. It was her worst fear, that Meghan could be dead. She didn't know how she'd survive it—

"Hey," Quinn said, gently snapping her out of her trance, "don't think the worst. Your sister's okay."

A tear escaped, despite Kerstin's best effort. "How would you know?"

A callused finger wiped the drop from her cheek.

The touch was somehow comforting and arousing, all mixed together. Added to her already jumbled state, she was more confused than ever.

"Do you feel she's dead?"

Kerstin shook her head. "No, I don't."

"Haley knew whenever her brother was in trouble. Which was a lot," he said with the beginning of a smile. "Theories abound about twins, and lots of them say that kind of link is hogwash, but I'm telling you I've seen it. It can be even stronger in identicals, don't you think?"

She cocked her head at him. "How'd you know Meghan and I are identical?"

Something flickered across his eyes, but Kerstin couldn't name it. Then he shrugged. "I didn't. I was just talking theory. Are you? Identical, I mean?"

"Yep. Mirror, actually."

"Mirror?"

"You know, I'm right-handed, she's left. I'm the logical, math-oriented one, she's the artistic free spirit." Kerstin giggled. "She even has her birthmark on her left side."

A smile tweaked the corner of his mouth. "No birthmark on Haley and her brother, but he was the artistic one, too. And the perpetual student."

"Not Meghan. She hated school. I loved it, but she thought it was too rigid. She cut more classes than she took. How she graduated at all is still a miracle. And I'm talking high school!"

Quinn chuckled with her, and when he laughed, his

dimples transformed him again to the mischievous man who'd whisked her out of Daddy's bar.

Her humor lagged a bit when the question of how he'd known she and Meghan were identicals nagged at her. She realized she dwelled too much on little details lately, but she was still sure she hadn't told him. And he had known, despite his denial.

She took a long look at his open, smiling face and let it go. Heaven knew she'd seen enough coincidences in the past few months to make her believe in the oddest things. Truth really was stranger than fiction, especially considering where she was at the moment. Who would have guessed she'd be under the protection of one of the roughest men in Hell, clucked over by a hardened biker as if she were a motherless chick?

As though he read her thoughts, Quinn asked, "You haven't told me the story about how you hooked up with Daddy yet. It has to be a whopper."

A flush crept up her neck, and Kerstin silently cursed it. She was too auburn to be a redhead, technically, but she was cursed with the fair skin and tendency to blush at the slightest provocation.

"It's a pretty stupid story."

Their order arrived, forcing a pause in the conversation as they scooped salsa over their eggs and ate. When she finally put her napkin on her plate and pushed it away, Quinn said, "I'm not letting you off the hook. Tell me."

"Well," she said, stalling by finishing her orange

juice, "my sister has always been attracted to the rough—"

She stopped abruptly, remembering who she was talking to. Or rather, what kind of guy she was talking to. She cleared her throat. "Um, she was always drawn to bikers. She's even had several biker... aficionados...as boyfriends, so when I heard she was in trouble, I knew where I should start looking."

She didn't know whether to cheer or curse the fact that Jackson Pepper had a reputation for his Harleys. If she ever found the group Pepper hung out with, his penchant for classic choppers might make him easier to find. The trick was finding the gang at all. The thought that she'd never catch up with the elusive bikers terrified Kerstin all the more.

But Quinn didn't need to know those details.

"And how did that bring you to Daddy's?"

"I was abominably stupid, actually. I was trying to find Meghan's last boyfriend, and a pal of his told me I could find him at Daddy's. Like a fool, I just walked into the place and asked for him. Daddy saved me from...um...some pretty rough treatment by knocking together the heads of the guys who were hassling me." She gave him a rueful smile. "You might have noticed that Daddy is good at head-knocking."

Quinn chuckled. "I noticed."

"Anyway, he told me I was a stupid...well, a not-nice name, and made me tell him my story. Then, and

I still have no idea why, he told me to park my trailer in his carport, and he gave me a job. He said he'd help find the information I needed, without my getting myself killed, or worse, before I was through.''

''And you trusted him?''

The red was back in her cheeks. ''Yeah, I did. My instincts said he wouldn't hurt me or he'd have never helped me in the first place. Besides, I was desperate at that point and I was willing to risk anything to find Meghan.''

Quinn hitched a foot on the rung of the chair next to him and draped an arm over the back of his seat. ''You certainly aren't stupid, Kerstin,'' he said sternly, ''but you are incredibly naive.''

''Thanks for the vote of confidence.''

He cocked his head and sent her an indulgent glance. She returned a sheepish shrug.

''Okay, so it wasn't so smart, but it turned out to be the right move. Daddy treats me like I'm his child or something. It's the weirdest thing...''

Quinn's brow furrowed. ''You said he treats you like his daughter...''

Shaking her head, Kerstin laughed again. ''No, don't even think it. I'm very much aware of who my parents are. They're in a retirement village in Hot Springs, Arkansas.'' Her face lost all its animation. Maybe it was a blessing in disguise that her mom remembered little these days. Her dad was still sharp mentally, but his heart was fragile, and she feared this was going to be too much for him. ''They're not in very good health. This whole thing with Meghan, this guy Pepper—''

"Pepper? Jackson Pepper?''

Kerstin jerked herself upright. Smiling too brightly, she pushed out of her chair. "Um, I've got to go to the ladies' room. I'll be right back.''

At the lavatory a moment later, she pounded a fist against the counter. What was wrong with her? Had she learned nothing over these past hellacious weeks? She had to keep her mouth shut around people Daddy hadn't okayed.

But Quinn so easily made her forget the need to hold her cards close to the vest. She didn't like how easily she'd fallen under his charm. She couldn't imagine what harm it could do to tell him about Meghan, but then again, she couldn't imagine what good it would do, either. She had to be careful, for Meghan's sake, and until she knew more about him, the less he knew the better.

Kerstin wrung out a cool towel and pressed it to her forehead, admonishing herself to keep her wits about her. She turned away from her reflection and took a few minutes to collect herself before she went back to the table.

Quinn took advantage of the time Kerstin was away to berate himself for being a fool. He had to get a hold of his impatience before he blew it. If he kept this up, all he was going to succeed at was losing his best lead. If he had any brains at all, he needed to change the subject, get her talking about herself and work on earning her trust.

He ignored the twitch of his conscience. Now was not the time to second-guess his plan. He needed to find Pepper and, at the moment, Kerstin was his most likely chance to succeed. She had a network of people looking for her sister, a network he could tap into if he was careful. Meghan had committed no crime as far as the Rangers knew, and she was with Pepper of her own free will, so Kerstin's sister wasn't his priority—or so he tried to tell himself. Somehow he doubted that would ease his conscience if she got hurt while he took Pepper down, though. All he could do was try to minimize the impact on Kerstin and Meghan, although how he was going to accomplish that, he had no idea.

When Kerstin returned to the table, he smiled congenially, forcing himself to stay seated. Quinn O'Byrne, biker, wouldn't stand when a lady came back to her seat, but Quinn O'Byrne, Texas Ranger and Southern gentleman, always had. Since he had much more experience in the latter role, it was one of the habits he monitored so he wouldn't blow his cover.

He looked at Kerstin, hiding his musings. He wondered how she thought she was pulling off this "biker babe" act. Every feature on her delicate face, every line of her slender body, every gesture from her graceful fingers screamed class. Her outfit was as incongruous on her as a dress would be on him.

He marshaled his wandering thoughts. "So, what did you do before you decided to take up waitressing in seedy bars?"

Kerstin looked up, obviously startled. "What?" She blushed. "I'm sorry, I was lost in my own little world for a minute."

He repeated the question.

"I worked for a brokerage firm in Austin. Still work, actually. I'm on leave."

He knew that, of course, but he played along. "I can see you as a broker," he said, eyeing the sleeveless vest which revealed such delicious portions of her skin, "even in that outfit."

The flush deepened on her cheeks. "Thanks, I think. But I'm not a broker. I'm the assistant to the senior broker."

She pulled her shoulders back proudly. Quinn doubted she was aware of the gesture.

"I will be, though," she continued. "I've been going to night school, and I should get my certification in about a year."

"Congratulations. In the meantime, what does a broker's assistant do?"

"Well, I flag the firm's files for review at different times, offering my ideas about what we should invest in next on their behalf. Some clients are very involved, some let us handle their portfolios." She smiled. "Of course, Mr. Henson doesn't always take my suggestions, but that's okay."

"How did you get started in investing? Did you

know you wanted to be a stockbroker when you were a little girl?''

She laughed, as he'd hoped his teasing tone would make her.

''No, I wanted to be the first woman president.'' She tilted her head sideways and made a funny grimace. ''Then I found out you had to be a politician.''

Quinn chuckled. ''I can see how that would disillusion an intelligent mind. So then you thought, 'I think I'll play with other people's money,' instead?''

''Oh, I play with my own, too. That's how I know I'm going to be good at this.''

He kept his thoughts to himself about what he'd like her to play with. He wasn't generally a crude man, but his body had gone on full-scale alert from the moment he'd set eyes on her. He could attribute his reaction to feeling alive again for the first time in a year, but he refused to label the awakening as anything except pure sexual attraction. His need for revenge and his duty to Haley's spirit had stripped his emotions of any civilized sentiments. He would confess to lust, but would not allow thoughts of anything softer. Not until Pepper was dead.

He struggled to remember where their conversation had paused. ''I'm sure you'll be a terrific broker,'' he finally said, feeling his answer lame, but what was he supposed to say?

''What keeps you in Hell?''

Her question turned the tables on him, and he wasn't prepared. His insides lurched.

Many things, darlin', many things, was what he wanted to say, but instead he answered, "I thought I'd meet up with…someone here. The guy hasn't shown yet, so I figured I'd hang out a little longer."

"Is your friend expecting you?"

Yeah, he was a friend all right. "No, this would be a surprise. I haven't seen him in a long time, and since I had time to…kill, I was taking the chance on finding him and going on a little road trip."

"What's his name? Maybe I've seen him at Daddy's."

Quinn thought fast. "Probably not. Thanks, though."

"Are you sure?"

"Hey, the wind's really picking up out there. Rain must be coming. I'd better get you to your trailer before we both get soaked."

"Okay," she said, obviously confused by his abrupt change of subject.

He tried to smooth the awkward moment by smiling as he paid the tab and escorted her back to his bike. "Thanks for coming to breakfast with me. I enjoyed the conversation and the company."

"Me, too," she said, stroking the motorcycle's tank with her fingers. "You have a beautiful bike. I have to confess that I much prefer the suspension on this to a fork-mounted ride."

"So, now you're not only an investment broker, you're a bike expert, too?" he teased.

"Oh, hardly an expert. I've picked up a little bit of the lingo, though."

The wind caught her laughter and carried it away. He hurried her back to Daddy's and walked her to her trailer just as the clouds loosed a downpour.

Quinn accepted the jacket she handed back to him and slipped it on, the lining still warm from her body. He clamped down fiercely on his imagination and flipped up the collar. For what good it would do, he mused, watching water sheet off the roof. Maybe getting good and wet, as well as cold, would stifle his raging hormones. And maybe it would ease the guilt eating him inside out.

"I guess I'd better go. Thanks again."

"Wait!" she said, and he thought he heard surprise in her voice, as if she'd been startled to hear herself, too.

He turned back.

"Why don't you come in and have a cup of coffee or something? The storm's moving pretty fast. It should blow over in a few minutes, and there's no sense in you getting drenched."

This woman was definitely much too softhearted to be stuck in Hell.

He glanced at the open door to Daddy's house, a screen keeping bugs out, yet letting noise in. He could hear the television overriding, but not obscuring, the snores coming from the easy chair just out of sight.

Some guard you are, he thought with a sudden, unexpected anger. Kerstin was so vulnerable, and she hadn't the vaguest idea just how. He prayed Daddy's reputation was enough to keep Kerstin unharmed until he could get her away.

Wait a minute! Where had that come from? He wasn't ''getting'' Kerstin anywhere. He was here for information and then he was gone. Period. Gone to find Pepper. Kerstin would just have to get her own self out of trouble.

''So, do you want some coffee or not?''

Quinn jerked himself back to the present. ''That'd be great.''

He followed her up the metal steps into a tiny pull-trailer. A bench seat was settled under a narrow window, and he could see a table on hinges designed to be raised to eat on. A miniature refrigerator and a two-burner stove separated the seating area from a curtain undoubtedly hiding a bed from sight. He wasn't an overly tall man, just six feet, but he felt like he was in a dollhouse. The place was spotlessly clean, which didn't surprise him. He'd already decided that Kerstin was the make-the-bed-before-leaving-the-house kind of woman. He tried to remember the last time he'd made a bed. Haley had always complained about that....

Kerstin busied herself at the tiny sink and started a drip percolator. She took a seat next to him on the bench, but scooted as far to the wall as she could. He could see she'd gone nervous on him again and was probably regretting her impulsive invitation.

He gave the trailer a deliberate once-over. "There's no place like home, huh?"

She shrugged. "It's dry, so I don't complain. I am anxious to get back to my house and my stuff, though. You know what I mean?"

He nodded. "Yeah, I do. I have a place out in the hill country, and I get antsy to be home if I'm on the road too long."

"What do you do...for a living, I mean?"

It was always best to stick as close to the truth as possible when telling lies. "If I'm not fixing bikes, I'm usually training horses."

She couldn't contain her surprise. "Horses?"

"Horses," he repeated, laughter bubbling in his voice. "Four-hoofed or two-wheeled, I like to ride."

Her blush was clear even in the poor light cast by the lamp attached to the wall. "I didn't mean to insult you. I just never would have thought..."

"What? Aren't bikers allowed hobbies?"

"Oh, sure, it's just you don't seem...I mean... you... Never mind."

"No, you opened this can of worms. I don't seem what?"

She scratched the side of her neck nervously. "You don't seem like you'd take the time to ride horses. When no one is watching, you get this look on your face like you're a man on a mission and no one can stop you. The picture you just painted doesn't match. Long, fast motorcycle rides, yes. Long, peaceful rides on a horse, no."

He didn't correct her that long, fast rides in a saddle were common—for him, at least. The woman was definitely too insightful as it was without giving her more fuel for her imagination. He'd better be doubly careful. And he'd better guide the subject onto another path.

"I have to blame my Irish parents for it, then."

"Are you really Irish? Or is this more blarney?"

He smiled at her skepticism and shook his head.

"It's the honest truth. My father was Irish by descent. My mother is from the auld sod," he said in his best brogue.

She smiled, delight lightening the strain around her eyes.

"You do that very well."

"I thank ya'. Sure and I miss Gran, too. I need to go over to the Isle soon and give 'er a kiss."

"Your mother lives in Ireland?"

He dropped the accent as he nodded. "My father died while I was in high school. She stayed long enough to see me get into college before she went home. She was lost in this country without Dad, and I understood."

"No siblings?"

He shook his head.

A brilliant flash of lightning and a loud clap of thunder made Kerstin jump.

"Hey," he said. "It's all right."

But his hand on her knee only made her jump again.

She smiled tremulously. "I hate to feel so stupid. Storms scare me badly."

He frowned at her. "You've said that several times now. I don't want you to call yourself stupid ever again, do you hear me?"

He moved his hand to the curve of her neck and stroked his thumb along her jawline. Her skin felt like silk under his fingertips. Hot, living silk.

He swallowed. Hard. "Lots of people are afraid of storms."

"I know, but I'm a grown woman. I should get over it."

Was it his imagination, or did her voice sound husky, deeper? And she was most certainly a grown woman. He could testify to the maturity in her full curves, the long sleek lines of her muscles, the desire calling out to him.

Her eyes were locked with his and sound became distorted. All he could hear was the rasp of his breath and the matching tenor of hers. It seemed the most natural thing in the world to let his fingers slip behind her neck to pull her to him gently, inexorably, until their mouths met.

All rational thought fled. Her eyes fluttered shut and a sweet sigh brushed across his face. She met him willingly, but with a tentative exploration that nearly undid him. Her touch screamed innocence, but he could not stop himself from delving into the velvet recesses of her mouth to coax her into a gentle battle of lips and tongues.

Minutes later, or possibly forever, he forced himself away from her bewitching taste. His body tormented him, calling him a fool for giving up so tempting an offer.

Once the contact was broken, Kerstin jerked back, her face flaming. She put her hands to her mouth, and Quinn's heart clenched at the embarrassment he saw in her eyes.

"Oh, my," she whispered. "I can't believe I did—"

"Kerstin," he said, trying to drag air into his starved lungs. "I'm...I'm sorry. I shouldn't have—"

"No," she said, jumping up to fiddle with the coffeepot, her fingers trembling. "You didn't...I mean, I—"

Quinn stood and took a step behind her and turned her to face him. "Kerstin, I'm sorry," he repeated. "I didn't mean for that to happen."

The agony in her eyes told him he'd chosen his words badly. God help him, he was so tired of saying the wrong thing, of doing the wrong thing, of failing....

"Listen to me," he said, pulling her infinitesimally closer, "I've wanted to kiss you since the moment I first saw you. But I didn't mean to rush you. Things have happened so fast."

"I don't know what's gotten into me. I feel so foolish."

"And I told you to stop saying that. I'm flattered

you lost your head. And maybe, sometime later, I can convince you to lose it again.''

As he hoped, she gave him a timid smile. He stepped back and put what little space he could between them.

''The rain has stopped. I should leave.''

She nodded. ''I think that might be best.''

He paused as he descended the steps and looked back at her. ''Don't give up hope, Kerstin. We'll find your sister.''

Then he was gone. Kerstin listened to the sound of his motorcycle fading into the early-morning darkness and closed up her trailer. She slipped into a nightgown, wondering what he'd meant by *we'll* find Meghan....

Later, as she tossed and turned on her bed, she realized her restlessness had little to do with the weather and a lot to do with a complete stranger who had come into her life like a flash of lightning and turned her already chaotic world on its edge.

Three

Quinn was away from Daddy's for several days running down clues. He was frustrated and saddle-sore when he finally made it to the parking lot. It seemed unusually crowded for a Thursday evening.

He had the small satisfaction of knowing Kerstin noticed exactly when he walked in. Her back was to him, but he saw her straighten and slowly turn her head to meet his eyes, as if she'd felt his presence...and his concentration on the cutoffs molding her hips in a most enticing fashion.

As he made his way across the room, he decided he was going to have to accept that Kerstin would always look out of place here. It didn't matter at what angle he viewed her—from the back where his eyes followed her shiny hair down to trace her spine and over the curve of her bottom; from the side, where her profile was porcelain enough to be painted by a great artist, her flat stomach peeking temptingly from under the edge of her vest, and her shorts a mere prelude to a mouthwatering length of leg; or her front, where her elegant throat seemed to cry out for a choker laced with pearls and diamonds, her leather vest more suitably replaced with a satin gown and her feet more appropriately shod in slippers.

Quinn shook his head at his own thoughts. Kerstin had a point—maybe he should stick to clichés. He was beginning to sound like a love-starved teenager who'd read too much Shakespeare. Or maybe not enough Shakespeare...

He could not forget his reason for being in this picturesque little town, and it was not to rescue Kerstin...no matter how pretty a picture she made of a damsel in distress. He certainly was no knight in shining armor, and he'd do well to hammer that into his pea brain. Damsels needed men of virtue and honor, not burned-out lawmen with murder on their minds.

Grabbing a beer from the bar, he took his customary seat. Kerstin was busy with a crowd near the pool table, so he made himself comfortable and watched her. She laughed at a joke he couldn't hear, and pulled a wandering hand off her hip. Her accompanying frown was just severe enough to make the guy realize she wasn't kidding.

Which was a good thing, considering the tightening

in Quinn's gut as he watched the traveling fingers. He was just about to come out of the booth and do a little impressionistic artwork on the guy's face when Kerstin made her reprimand. Quinn forced himself to stay put and hoped his indolent pose looked believable.

His displeasure turned to amusement at Kerstin's studious avoidance of his table. He didn't hurry, but when he finished his beer, he caught her eye and lifted the bottle to signal her.

She finally made her way over with his order.

"Busy night," he said, making sure his inane comment was accompanied by a teasing smile.

Her glance around the room took longer than necessary. "I guess."

He tipped his head toward her hands. "It's really all right with me if you leave the label on."

Kerstin flushed furiously when she realized she was scratching the paper off the bottle. She slammed it down, pivoting to leave.

"Hang on a second." He pulled his wallet out and paid for his drink. When she reached for the money, he caught her wrist. "We need to talk."

She shook her head. "There's nothing to say. I appreciate your offer, but I'm doing fine on my own."

"We haven't even discussed what I might be able to do for you."

"It doesn't matter."

Her beautiful lips firmed, and a hardness came over her eyes.

"You're telling me that even if I might be able to

help you find your sister, you're going to go bull-headed on me and refuse?''

She narrowed her eyes at him, but he knew he'd hit a button.

"I am not being bullheaded," she said, "and I really don't have time to talk right now."

He quirked an eyebrow at her. He wasn't letting her off the hook. "Oh, I think you can spare me a few minutes."

She gave him an exasperated sigh before sitting down across from him as though the bench might bite her.

"Look, Quinn, I appreciate your offer—"

"Kerstin, what's the real problem? Everything about you says you're the kind of person who is logical and uses excellent judgment. Why are you being so foolish now?"

A flash of the fear she kept so tightly reined danced across her face. "This whole situation is upside down!"

She caught herself and lowered her voice. "The people I should trust, I can't. And the people I shouldn't trust are the only ones I can turn to."

He pretended confusion. "What do you mean?"

Kerstin ran a wary hand over her eyes. "You already know my sister is with a guy named Jackson Pepper. I found out that he's a drug dealer and probably a murderer."

"How did you find that out?" he asked with just the perfect note of curiosity.

The two voices at war in his head piped up. One told him to stay the course, to keep his cover firmly in place. The other part, the vestiges of his once strong moral compass, berated him for leading her on with his sins of omission.

He reminded the wavering part of himself that revenge had fed him and fueled him for a long time now, keeping him alive and fighting when guilt and grief had made him want to curl up into a ball and die. He could not—he would not—give in to the urge to soften his stance. It would not only betray his vow to Haley, but a loss of focus could get them all killed—Kerstin, Meghan, himself. He had a job to do, a promise to keep.

"It doesn't matter how I know. What's important is this guy is going to hurt my sister. He may even kill her if I don't find her soon."

Quinn hid his disappointment when she didn't reveal the whole story. He knew if he could get her to open up, half the battle would be won. She was wavering, that much he could tell, but if he pushed too hard, she'd close up again. He had to gain her trust…and time was against them both.

"So you see, Quinn, I can't afford to take any more chances. I think I've already used up my quota of good luck. This is my sister's life we're talking about, and I have to stay strong, stay focused. For Meghan's sake."

She clenched her fingers together so tightly he heard her knuckles pop, and met his eyes for a brief moment. He read a mixture of longing and regret before she seemed to focus on his lips. The image of her mouth against his bloomed in his mind, and without a word, he knew she was remembering their kiss just as he was.

He had to strain to hear her when she began again.

"You made me forget why I'm here, even if only for a moment, and I can't repeat that mistake."

He took her hand in his. "Kerstin—"

A bottle pounded against a table, and a voice boomed across the room, "Hey! Where's my beer?"

Kerstin jerked her wrist from his grasp. "I've got to go."

Quinn didn't stop her. With anxiety eating at him, the evening dragged on. He finally accepted an invitation for a game of pool to break the monotony, to ease the boredom of waiting.

Two games later, he still had to force himself to concentrate. He chalked his cue and studied the table, deciding between cutting the seven into the side or trying the long shot for the three in the corner. Bending over, he lined up his angle.

What he needed was the right angle to get Kerstin talking again. He was so close—

"You playin' pool or communin' with the dead?"

Quinn didn't let Lucky's grousing get to him. Lucky was just ticked because he was down a hundred bucks.

Glancing around, Quinn saw Kerstin had paused in delivering her tray to the corner. He felt his lip twitch despite his best efforts to appear as though he hadn't noticed her glance toward his backside. Not that he wasn't flattered, of course, but if he wanted another fifty of Lucky's money, he'd best keep his mind on pool and not the appreciation he'd seen in Kerstin's eyes. If he dwelled on the hungry sensuality she was trying so valiantly to hide, he'd lose his concentration and—

"Hell and creation, Irish, you gonna shoot it or ask it to marry you?"

The seven dropped into the pocket. Quinn cut Lucky a look and returned his attention to the cue ball. With precise execution, the three shot into the corner.

The eight was an easy sink, and Lucky swore as he reached for the wallet attached to his jeans by a length of chain.

Quinn knew when to tease Lucky and when to let the man stew. Right now, Lucky probably needed a pinch of salt and dash of garlic....

While he waited for his opponent to grab a fresh beer, Quinn racked the balls.

"Don't beat him too many times in a row."

Quinn turned around and faced Kerstin. He was touched by the concern etched on her features.

"Worried about me?"

"No," she denied with obvious prevarication. "I'm worried about you getting blood on that felt. I'm the one who'd have to clean it."

He reached out and stroked the corner of her

mouth. He wasn't sure who was more surprised by his spontaneous gesture, but he wasn't going to let the moment go to waste. Instinct told him to be sincere.

"Thanks, Kerstin," he said softly. "I'll be okay."

She flushed. "It's just…I mean…Lucky's had a lot to drink."

She moved away with a rare awkwardness. Quinn turned back to the table when Lucky reappeared, vaguely noticing the door opening out of his peripheral vision. He didn't let a booming laugh interfere with his break, and he watched with satisfaction as a stripe and a solid landed in pockets on opposite sides of the table.

Quinn had a vague sense of a missile hurtling toward him just as a foghorn laugh sounded in his ear.

"Irish!"

Quinn turned in time to catch a leather-clad blonde as she cast herself into his arms. He was thankful for the support of the pool table because it was clear Cindy had no sense of physics, or that she had a little more mass than the last time they'd met. Quinn was sure he was going to have a bruise across his hip at the exact height of the table lip.

Cindy reached up and yanked his head down. He barely managed to shift his mouth to catch the corner of her lips and avoid the full benefit of her affection. It wasn't that he didn't like Cindy, it was more that he didn't tend to be so openly…affectionate.

To avoid hurting her feelings, Quinn pulled her into

a fierce hug, girding himself to swing her around before setting her on her feet.

He caught Kerstin's eye, and was glad Cindy's back was toward his petite defender. Cindy was known for her right hook, but Quinn wasn't so sure she would be the odds-on favorite against the look on Kerstin's face.

"Hey, Irish, how the hell are you?"

"Herniated, but happy. And you?"

"You know me, Irish. I'm always good."

Despite the obvious insinuation in her tone, Quinn didn't know her well enough to confirm or deny the claim. But he did know Kerstin had heard, and he wasn't sure if he should be flattered or amused by the straightening of her shoulders.

Lucky's patience ran out. "Listen—"

"Here, Lucky," Quinn said, slapping the fifty he'd just won on the felt. "Let me skip out of this game. I'm gonna buy the lady a drink."

Lucky grabbed the money. "Sure, sure," he said with a now-magnanimous smile. "We'll go again later."

Cindy's foghorn let loose again. "Lucky still a piss-poor shot?"

"He's improving."

"Liar."

Quinn just grabbed his beer and smiled, escorting her to his table...if you could call walking behind the woman's swagger an escort.

"So, what brings you here? Where's your old man?"

"He'll be here in a minute. He's checking his clutch cable. It was slipping on the way down."

"Down from…?"

"Oklahoma City. We spent some time with friends up there."

"Where are you headed now?"

"North Houston. There's a big rally this weekend. Didn't you know that? I bet half the folks in here are headed that way."

Quinn shook his head, hoping Jim, Cindy's long-time partner, would join them soon. Discussing the rally would be the perfect opportunity to bring up Pepper. They made a career out of Harley rallies and were a rich source of information.

Jim came in shortly, a big grin animating his boyish face. He didn't look like a stereotypical biker. He was tall and gangly, and had a head of red hair that needed a dimmer switch. His grip as he shook hands with Quinn revealed a strength belied by his wiry build.

"Hey, Irish. You trying to move in on my old lady?"

Quinn grinned back and motioned Jim to sit. "Nah. I kinda like my face arranged the way it is."

The three laughed at the weak joke just as Kerstin moved to stand beside the table. Before she could speak, Cindy's eyes grew big.

"Meghan!" she bellowed, causing both men and

Kerstin to wince. "What are you doing here? How did you beat us down from Oklahoma City?"

"I'm not—"

"Not that I'm not glad you're away from that piece of scum, but—"

"Cindy, wait!" Quinn interrupted, signaling her to stop. "This isn't Meghan. This is her sister, Kerstin."

Kerstin had grown pale. Quinn pulled her down onto the bench beside him and put an arm around her shoulders.

"Are you all right?" he asked, chafing her fingers between his hands.

She nodded, but looked at Cindy. "You've seen my sister?"

Cindy gave her a quizzical glance and then let out her signature bullhorn laugh. "Come on, you guys. I'm not falling for this."

"I'm serious—" Quinn began.

"I really am Meghan's sister," Kerstin piped in. "I've been looking for her for weeks now. Please, when did you see her?"

Cindy shot Jim a look. He shrugged.

Kerstin let out an exasperated sigh. "I'm not Meghan. See—" She shifted her vest to reveal the birthmark on her hip peeking over the edge of her waistband. "My birthmark is on the right side. I'm right-handed. Meghan's left-handed, and her birthmark's on her left hip. Assuming you've seen her birthmark, of course."

Cindy squinted her eyes while she thought. "You're right! Hey, you two twins or something?"

Quinn rolled his eyes at Cindy's power of deduction, earning a faint smile from Kerstin.

Kerstin confirmed the obvious and sat forward in her seat. "Please, I need to know everything you can tell me about the last time you saw Meghan."

"Like I told Irish, we've been up in Oklahoma City. That was about a week ago. She's traveling with a guy named Pepper." Cindy shifted uncomfortably. She looked at Jim, but again, he simply shrugged.

"Look, I don't know if I should tell you this," she said, glancing at Quinn, back at Jim, and then to Kerstin, "but this Pepper dude is bad news."

Despite the excitement he felt at this first real lead, Quinn's heart constricted at the pain he saw in Kerstin's eyes.

Cindy reached across the table and put her fingers over Kerstin's. "I'm real sorry. I was hoping you were Meghan. That's why I was so excited. I thought you'd...I mean, she'd gotten away. She's real sweet."

Quinn watched Kerstin and steeled his heart, forcing himself not to give in to the part of himself that wanted to protect her, to shield her from any more distressing information.

"Do you know which direction Pepper was heading?" he asked, keeping his hand on Kerstin's arm, but not looking her way.

"I think they're headed for the same rally in North Houston, like us. But I'm not sure."

"North Houston?" Kerstin asked.

Cindy named a big field known for hosting events like this, and Jim sketched directions for her.

"Thanks," Kerstin said as she slid out of the booth. "I really appreciate this. But if you'll excuse me, I've got some things to do."

Quinn watched her walk over to the bar. She spoke to Daddy, her hands moving animatedly. Daddy shook his head, but a determined set came into Kerstin's shoulders.

"Listen, Irish, I hope—"

Quinn was already sliding out of his seat, jacket in hand. He threw Cindy a salute.

"Thanks for the info. See ya 'round, okay?"

He didn't wait for a reply. His attention was on Daddy, who had just followed Kerstin out the back door. He quickened his steps and caught the screen before it banged shut.

"Kerstin," the big man called out.

Quinn was surprised when she stopped her determined march to her trailer.

"You're not going to that rally alone," Daddy said.

"You can't stop me," she said determinedly. Then she seemed to lose some of the starch in her spine. She took a step toward Daddy and managed a tremulous smile. "Daddy, you've been a great help to me, and I appreciate all you've done. But I've got to go, you know that."

Daddy shook his head. "It's too dangerous—"

"I'll take her," Quinn interrupted before another futile exchange began.

Daddy and Kerstin whirled to look at him.

"What?" Kerstin asked, staring at him as though he'd grown a third eye.

"I said I'd—"

"I heard you," she snapped, frowning. "Didn't you hear what I said earlier?"

"I heard."

"Then why are you out here?" she asked, planting her fists on her hips. "This isn't any of your business."

"I'm making it my business not to let you go off half-cocked and get yourself into God-knows-what kind of trouble. You don't know your way around a rally any more than I know my way around a stock exchange."

Kerstin's face took on the stubborn look he was beginning to recognize. "I can't trust you. I don't even know you!"

A shout erupted from within the bar and Daddy stepped forward, obviously torn. With a growl, he jabbed a beefy finger into Quinn's chest. "Don't do anything stupid."

Quinn let the challenge go and moved closer to Kerstin as Daddy headed into the bar to investigate the problem. As they had during their first conversation, Quinn and Kerstin found themselves alone behind Daddy's Place.

"Kerstin—"

"The answer is still no. I can't stop you from following me, but I'm heading out of here on my own."

Quinn struggled with his anger at her foolishness. He should just leave her. What did he care? He had a solid lead and he didn't need the hassle of keeping an eye on her....

He cooled his temper. If the lead didn't pan out and he lost contact with Kerstin, he could really be up a creek.

"Look," he said, taking a deep breath, "I can help you."

The back door burst open, and two men came barreling out. Daddy was close behind, carrying his bat.

One of the men careened into Quinn, latching on for balance. When the man straightened and stepped away, he did a double take, and his already angry face turned ugly.

With a roar, he launched himself back at Quinn.

Kerstin put her hand to her mouth and quelled a scream. She watched, stunned, as Quinn countered the man's clumsy swing with a sidestep, using the biker's momentum against him to send him crashing into the picnic table.

She glanced at Daddy, but he was busy encouraging the second man to stay out of the fray by presenting the broad end of his bat for inspection.

By the time she looked back at Quinn, he was taking his attacker down to the ground. It didn't take but a moment for Quinn to wrench the man's arm around and he finally lay still.

"What'd you do that for?" Quinn demanded.

Kerstin wanted to know the same thing. She looked at Quinn, noting his harsh breathing and the fierce expression on his face. At the moment, he didn't look like someone to argue with.

Her own heart was racing. The fear of Quinn being hurt had her posture so rigid her back hurt.

Quinn jostled the man's arm to solicit an answer.

After a string of expletives, the man tried to look over his shoulder at Quinn.

"You sold us out, you—"

Quinn used his knee to knock the breath out of the man before he could begin another session of foul language. "I don't know what you're talking about!"

"In Uvalde. You're one of the pigs who busted our shop about a year ago. A few of us got away. I saw you!" The man struggled uselessly under Quinn's grip.

"What's your name, man?" Quinn demanded.

It didn't appear he was going to answer, and then Kerstin heard a sullen, "Benji."

"Listen, Benji, I don't know who you think you saw, but it wasn't me."

To Kerstin, the man obviously didn't believe Quinn, but he quit struggling.

"If I let you up, will you stop this crap?"

Benji gave a grudging nod.

With a smooth move, Quinn stood, taking Benji's bowie knife from its holster as he backed away.

Kerstin glanced at Daddy, who was watching Quinn with an intensity that caught her attention. As she looked around at the other participants in this odd play, she felt as though she'd entered into the surreal.

She saw Quinn meet Daddy's eyes and the two men locked gazes for what seemed an eternity, as if they were sizing each other up. It made her anxious, for she knew she was the reason for the posturing.

Time snapped back into place as Daddy took a step toward Benji and his pal and growled, "You didn't see this guy in Uvalde."

It was clear Quinn had already created a suitable impression, but with Daddy's backup, fear replaced the sullen look in Benji's eyes. Kerstin was sure he didn't believe what he'd been told, but she was fairly sure he wasn't going to press the issue.

"Yeah, whatever."

Benji dusted off his jeans and nodded to his buddy. With one final bravado glare at Quinn, the two men left around the back of the building.

Daddy turned back to Quinn. "You need to get out of here. They'll be back. With friends."

Quinn nodded.

Daddy tipped his head her way, but kept looking at Quinn. "You know she's going to that rally no matter what I say."

Kerstin's temper flared. She despised it when men talked around her as though she wasn't there.

"Listen, you two—"

"Yeah, I know," Quinn answered Daddy.

"You do anything stupid and I'll hunt you down." Daddy issued his warning in a voice as soft as his deep bass would allow.

"I'll take care of her."

"You will not!" Kerstin stepped between the two men who'd obviously decided they were her keepers.

Quinn offered his hand to Daddy, his arm almost brushing her stomach, and she watched in amazement as the big man reached across her as well, shaking Quinn's hand.

A cold fury settled over Kerstin. Without another word to either barbarian, she turned on her heel and headed for her trailer. No matter how much she appreciated Daddy's help these past weeks, she would not allow anyone to treat her this way.

She wasn't prepared when Quinn caught her arm and stopped her, turning her to face him. Jerking her arm out of his grasp, she took a step back.

"Kerstin, listen—"

"No, you listen," she said, her voice even and low.

In an odd way, she was almost grateful to the two chauvinist pigs. She'd been stuck in a place of fear for what seemed like forever. Their behavior had helped to get her back to her center, to the core of determination that had set her on this mission in the first place.

"I don't know who either of you think you are," she said, noticing that Daddy had gone back into the bar, but she kept going, "but I am neither a puppet nor a child. I don't need your or anyone else's approval for what I do. For God's sake! I don't even know your last name, so don't go thinking you can tell me what to do."

"O'Byrne."

"What?"

"Quinn Patrick O'Byrne."

She couldn't help a sarcastic twist from curving her lips. "Pleased to meet you. Now go away."

"I'm not going away, Kerstin."

"Fine. Do whatever you want. Just leave me alone."

"I can't do that either."

Kerstin threw up her hands. "What is it with you? Why do you care what happens to me? Or my sister, for that matter. It's not like we're best friends, you know."

Quinn looked her dead in the eyes and what she saw there stopped her anger in its tracks. She saw a determination making her own seem like child's play. She saw a need, a cold, hard calculating zeal telling her no matter what she said, he wasn't leaving. The oddest part of it all was the glimpse of something she couldn't name, something ephemeral. It spoke directly to her heart, telling her in a clear, indisputable way that he was a good man and he had her care in mind, no matter what else he was thinking.

"I care," Quinn said, in a tone matching hers, "because of reasons I can't tell you about right now. We don't have time.''

He took a deep breath and ran his hands over his face before pinning her with his eyes again. ''Just as you trusted Daddy on your instincts, I'm asking you to trust me. Ride with me to the rally. I can help you look for your sister, and you'll blend in on my bike a whole lot better than in your truck.''

For a moment, she didn't know what to do. He had a valid argument—she'd had little success on her own. Kerstin knew she was an obvious wanna-be to the crowds she was trying to infiltrate, and Quinn carried himself with an air that let him into circles she could never break. He was asking her to trust him, a complete stranger. Yet she couldn't argue her trust in Daddy against all logic. And logic was now saying it couldn't hurt to travel with someone, and if nothing else, it made sense to have an extra set of eyes helping her look for Meghan, especially in a crowded place.

Please, she prayed, glancing skyward, tell me what to do.

Before she realized what she was doing, she nodded, and said, ''All right.''

Quinn smiled and gave her shoulder a warm squeeze. ''Get some clothes and whatever else you'll need. I'll go get my bike, and you can put your stuff in my saddlebags.''

She did as directed, knowing enough to pack the most minimal essentials with the limited space she'd have available. She had a feeling she'd be gone for a while so she took the last of the cash and her credit cards from their hiding place in the trailer. When her frantic movements were completed, she stood in the silence and looked around, wondering what in the world she was doing. This decision had a monumental feel.

Heaven help her if she'd made the wrong choice.

Four

Traveling by motorcycle gave him too much time to think, and he had to be careful not to get hypnotized by his headlight hitting the reflectors in the road. At least in a car he had the radio to keep his mind occupied. Maybe if he were a Gold Wing kind of guy he'd have a jack to plug a stereo into his helmet, but his Electra Glide boasted only a half-height faring, no jack on his helmet and no stereo in sight.

Needing desperately to keep his mind away from the feel of Kerstin's legs framing him from behind, he began to catalog his information about Pepper. Maybe anger would take the edge off this hyperawareness of Kerstin's touch.

Jackson Pepper had been linked to so many drug-

and homicide-related crimes in the past five years, they should have bypassed the trials and sent the man to the gas chamber without another thought. Since it appeared the bastard would never see justice in the courts, Quinn was just going to take care of Pepper's little payback to society. And to Haley.

God, did it have to hurt so much every time he thought about her?

It was easier to think about Pepper, to wonder how many counts of grand theft he had against him. How many trafficking in narcotics? How many murder and accessory to murder?

But what was the point? Regardless of how many counts, the only one that mattered was a murder-one indictment the scumbag had weaseled out of.

Damn it, Haley, I'm so sorry. It didn't help that things hadn't been so good between them those last couple of years. Knowing Haley had been increasingly lonely and sad made his guilt even heavier. The fact that he'd been thinking about divorce made it almost impossible to bear.

He tried to remember what his partner had said the last time they were together at headquarters. Something about if Pepper had chosen to be a religious nut instead of a drug runner, there'd be no stopping another Jonestown or Waco. Pepper had the charisma to attract countless followers.

He shook away the thoughts. They were irrelevant because Pepper wasn't a preacher-gone-psycho, he was a very sane, very evil man who'd chosen to thumb his nose at the law time after time. And Quinn had to stop him. Period.

Nearly being clipped by a Suburban forced Quinn to get his mind back on his driving. It was hard enough staying safe on the road as it was without letting his mind wander. He never failed to be amazed at the number of people who either simply didn't see motorcycles or paid them no attention. Then there were the aggressive jerks who got a kick out of forcing a bike off the road.

Kerstin carefully shifted on the seat behind him and a quick glance at his watch told him he'd been lost inside his head longer than he would have guessed. They'd been on the road for nearly two hours now. She hadn't once complained, but two hours on a bike for someone not used to riding—even one hour, for that matter—could be a long time. When he saw a sign for a rest stop, he took the exit and pulled over.

He felt a twinge of guilt when he noticed her valiant but not quite successful attempt at pretending she wasn't stiff.

"I'm sorry, Kerstin. I forget it's much easier to drive a motorcycle than be a passenger."

"I'm fine."

"Still, I—"

"I said I'm fine."

She pivoted and headed for the ladies' room, the vapor lights overhead making her seem washed-out and strained. At least, he hoped it was the lights.

Waving off a mosquito, Quinn watched her walk away, a puzzled frown on his face.

Had he done something wrong? Other than getting lost in thought, he couldn't imagine what had made her angry. Unless she'd gone back to feeling tricked into coming with him.

He sighed as he fed quarters into the machine and accepted his can of cola from the slot. He started to buy one for Kerstin, but she'd been wearing an expression that said no matter what he picked it wouldn't be what she wanted. Hopping up to sit on the end of a picnic table away from the lights and bugs, he let his legs dangle. He put his helmet beside him, grimacing at the face shield, and made a mental note to clean it before they hit the road again.

He took a sip of his not-quite-cold-enough drink and grimaced again, not sure if he should attribute the expression to the soda or the sudden thought that, if there was one redeeming facet of loneliness, it was being spared the "I'm mad at you and I'm not going to tell you why" game. Haley had been a master at it. Sides of beef could have stayed unspoiled in the house when she was on a tear.

Funny, he'd forgotten about that. It had driven him crazy. And he'd taken perverse delight in pretending it hadn't, which only made her angrier. In retrospect, he felt childish and regretted the time wasted in petty fights.

One thing was for sure, he wasn't going to put up

with it now. By the time Kerstin reappeared and reached the table, he was ready to take her on.

"Would you like a soda?" he asked, indicating his own choice.

"No, thank you. My bladder almost didn't make it here as it was."

"I said I was sorry about that. I'll be more conscious from now on."

"I'm a big girl. I should have said something sooner."

Quinn lifted his free hand in surrender. "Fine. Since that's settled, will you tell me what's got you riled?"

"Riled?" she repeated, her expression puzzled.

"You look like you're about to bust a gasket. What's on your mind?"

Kerstin sat on the tabletop a comfortable space away from him, but not the you're-scum-and-I'm-not-coming-near-you distance. That's encouraging, he thought.

He didn't rush her. He let her watch the people streaming in and out of the rest rooms, to and from tables to trash cans, in and out of cars. She seemed inordinately preoccupied with a collie puppy who didn't understand the leash law and the six- or seven-year-old little boy who kept trying to explain the problem of them going around different sides of a pole. The collie merely jumped to lick the youngster's nose with each verbal lesson.

He forced himself to stay seated, no matter how

badly he wanted to tell her to play her games if she wanted but to deal him out. He was rewarded when she gave a little sigh and turned her face toward him.

"I've had nothing to do but think for the past two hours, and I've found, without the distractions of Daddy and the bar, I've had some rather startling thoughts."

He waited. Then gave in. "And?"

"And I'm convinced you aren't telling me the truth. Or at least, you aren't telling me the whole story."

His gut meter red-lined, but he made sure his face didn't show it. "About what?"

She gave him a don't-pretend-you're-stupid-with-me smile. "Earlier, you said you had reasons you couldn't tell me about at the moment, so I think you know."

Okay, no playing innocent. He'd better try careful misdirection.

"Indulge me. Give me one more clue."

"You didn't come into Daddy's place by accident."

"Why do you say that?"

"Because you watched me like a hawk from the moment you walked in."

He tried for his come-on grin. "Ever think it's because you're about the sexiest thing in cutoffs around the place?"

Her blush was charming. It made a warm feeling curl up in his chest when her face took on that innocent, embarrassed expression. But his attempt at misdirection didn't work. Not that he'd actually expected it to.

"No, I don't think so. I have a feeling you've seen your share of cute girls' butts so I don't think there was anything extraordinary about mine. Besides, you didn't watch my butt. You watched my face."

"You have a beautiful face."

"Thank you. Now shut up."

He obeyed.

"The first couple of nights you were there, you tried to flirt with me, but there was never any real excuse for you to talk to me."

He stayed silent as ordered.

She rolled her eyes. "Then the fight broke out and you manhandled me out of there."

"I didn't manhandle you. I—"

She gave him *the look*.

"I know," he sighed. "Shut—"

"Up," she finished for him. "From that moment on, you've been my shadow. Don't get me wrong. Being a little ole female—" she made her voice breathless and put a limp hand to her heart "—I just admire a big, strong man wantin' to protect me."

She fluttered her lashes at him and despite his valiant effort, he laughed.

"Yeah, yeah," he said, "go on."

"You've asked a lot of questions for a stranger, and it didn't hit me until a while ago. Things just aren't meshing. I've trusted my instincts so far, and I believe your intent isn't to hurt me. But I do believe you have an agenda you're keeping hidden.''

"And if I keep it hidden?"

Kerstin shrugged. "That depends. You give me an explanation sounding remotely like the truth, and we'll keep traveling together. You don't, and I'm outa here."

"On what? We're at a rest stop and Houston is at least another hour from here."

"I can thumb it."

The thought of Kerstin hitchhiking in those tight jeans, a leather jacket and all that glorious hair made his blood run cold.

"You got a death wish?"

She gave him another don't-be-stupid look. "Every person who picks up a hitchhiker isn't a mass murderer, Quinn."

"It's a much safer rule of thumb these days." He smiled. "No pun intended."

She grimaced. "Of course not. And you're trying to change the subject."

He nearly smiled again. Damn, she sure had a lot of smarts packed into her little body.

"I'll make you a deal. Let's get on into Houston and find a place to stay for the night. If I don't tell you what you want to hear, you can head out fresh tomorrow."

"What if I think that'll give you too much time to come up with a cover story?"

"It's a risk you'll have to take."

Kerstin wasn't so sure she bought his bravado. He might not like it, but she did have choices. They might not be the most attractive of choices, but they were still hers to make. Finally she decided her best shot was to keep things as they were, for now. She batted away a fly and picked up her helmet.

"I'll take your deal. Let's go."

With the exception of taking time to clean his face shield and making another pit stop down the road, they made it into Houston by one o'clock. Even that late, the streets were still busy, and all the hotels close to the park were full. They headed another fifteen minutes down the highway before Quinn found a vacancy, and it was almost comically predictable to find only one room available. As he'd been prepared to bribe the clerk into saying exactly that, Quinn was delighted. He didn't want Kerstin out of his sight.

Kerstin was across the lobby, stretching the kinks out of her legs. He motioned her over.

"There's only one room, believe it or not, although it's a double. Do you want to keep going or can you handle sharing?"

"I can handle it. You may think I'm some helpless little kitten, but you'll regret it if you mess with me."

He didn't think she was helpless so much as prone to putting herself in harm's way. There were places even angels feared to tread, but he had the feeling Kerstin wasn't so cautiously inclined.

He didn't respond to the taunt, merely ignoring the money she held out and handed the clerk his credit card. He thought he caught the words *stubborn* and *caveman* from under her breath, but he didn't look up from signing the receipt. Despite her protests that she could do it herself, he carried both of their satchels in from the saddlebags.

The room, bearing the same clean-but-boring decor of midpriced hotels, was blessedly cool. Like most patrons, all they wanted was a shower and some sleep. He didn't argue when Kerstin told him he could have the bathroom first, even if it wasn't his most chivalrous move to date.

He was already under the covers, his hands stacked under his head since he'd been staring at the ceiling, when she came out some time later in an oversize T-shirt covering all the appropriate places, but leaving little to his imagination. She was rubbing her hair with a towel, oblivious to his eyes hungrily devouring her figure. Not that his imagination had needed much prompting since he'd first laid eyes on her, especially when he watched those long, silky legs…

She dropped her towel and shook her hair out of her face. The expression in her eyes, and the way her sexy mouth sort of moved without making a sound as she looked at his bare chest, did a lot of good for his ego. For propriety's sake, he was wearing underwear, but he wasn't about to wear a T-shirt to bed—innocent little, virgin-like Kerstin or not.

He watched, amused, as she contained herself and slid into her bed, pulling the covers from their tight corners and sitting comfortably against the headboard with a pillow fluffed in her lap.

Quinn rolled his head toward her and watched. She was oblivious to the enticing picture she made, and he was grateful for his concealing blankets. His body had already reacted to the pictures painted in his mind as he'd listened to the shower running, and doing his damnedest not to imagine Kerstin under the spray, the water slicking her hair back and turning it dark, the droplets cascading down her neck, over her breasts and down her flat stomach to—

"So, are you going to tell me what you're thinking or not?"

Most definitely not. Not unless he wanted his face slapped.

"You're partly correct about my reasons for being at Daddy's Place," he launched in, not pretending to misunderstand her opening foray. "I did know who you were, but I didn't know you were at Daddy's until I came in there."

"So you were looking for me."

"Sort of. I was looking for Meghan."

"You're looking for my sister? Why?" Even from across the room, he could feel her bristling like a porcupine.

"I don't want Meghan, per se." He felt the acid roil in his stomach. "I want Jackson Pepper."

"Why?"

"Because I knew from the word around that your

sister is with Jackson Pepper, and that you were look-ing for her.''

''Why are you after Pepper?''

''Trust me, Kerstin, you don't want to know. Just be satisfied that we're both after the same goal, we just want different people out of the deal. You want your sister, and it suits me just fine to help you find her.''

''That's not good enough.''

''It's going to have to be. Jackson Pepper is a cold-blooded murderer. He's run more dope through Texas in the past five years than you can imagine, and he's left a trail of dead or hurt women in his wake.''

''Then why haven't the police caught him.''

''Because he's also one smart son-of-a—'' He pulled himself up short. ''He's smooth, he's smart, and he has a sleezoid lawyer who also happens to be smart.'' Quinn rubbed his face with both hands.

He realized he was running off at the mouth and silently cursed himself, especially when he saw the look Kerstin was giving him.

''You know a lot about Pepper,'' she said, her brow furrowed.

''I've made it my business to find out about him.''

Please, please, let her buy it and leave it alone.

''Did you talk with the Texas Rangers, too? They came to my house asking about Meghan and told me a little about him.''

Talk about a gift horse...

''Yeah, as a matter of fact, I did.''

"They didn't tell me much." She made a face. "Must be because I'm a delicate little woman and couldn't handle the big details."

"Or maybe the guy was trying to be nice and not scare the pants off of you. Does every man have to have a negative motive with you?"

She ignored his question. "It's possible he was trying to be nice, but if I'd known in the beginning what you know, I might be closer to finding Meghan than I am."

"And you might be closer to dead. Did you ever consider that the Ra—the cops didn't expect you to go off half-cocked and chasing after a killer?"

"And what was I supposed to do? Sit at home and twiddle my thumbs, trusting my sister's life to a bunch of yahoos who can't even convict the man? That Ranger told me to my face they can't even look for Meghan because she's not kidnapped. She went with Pepper voluntarily. Like that'll matter if she's dead."

He forced down the urge to defend the Rangers and the other agencies who'd fared no better at nailing Pepper. He wasn't going to get into an argument that lawmen didn't do the convicting anyway, juries did.

He got control of his emotions. "It all boils down to the fact that I'm your best shot for finding Meghan, and you're not going to blow this chance just because you're curious. You know it, and I know it."

"Don't be so sure, mister. You're not the only biker who's offered to help me."

"But I am the only one with the time and inclination to run you around Texas following hunches. And I don't expect anything out of you in return."

Her blush this time was not so endearing as the last. They both knew he was right. Some perverse part of him—tired of games, tired of searching, tired of it all—ground out, "Unless you'd like to make a little exchange for my efforts."

Kerstin threw an ashtray at him and he barely deflected it from hitting his temple. Her eyes were blazing.

"You can go to hell, Quinn. Whatever you're angry about, don't take it out on me."

He forced his pulse to calm. He sat up, dragging his sheet with him, and put the ashtray back on the nightstand dividing the two beds.

He waited a moment before looking up at her. "I apologize, Kerstin. I'm generally not a crude man. I don't know what got into me."

She obviously believed his sincerity for the anger drained out of her posture. After giving a weary sigh, she opened her eyes. "It's all right. If I had to hazard a guess, I'd say fatigue has gotten into you. I'm so damned tired of searching, of waiting, of wanting to know if my sister is dead or alive…it…it makes me short-tempered sometimes, too."

"You're experiencing what a friend of mine calls an emotional whiteout."

"Don't you mean blackout?"

"No," Quinn answered, ignoring the urge to invite

her over to his bed so he could work the kinks out of those delicate shoulders. "He says an emotional blackout is true, deep depression. A whiteout is when you're just numb. You keep functioning, but you're a blank sheet of paper."

Kerstin raised an eyebrow as she nodded. "That sounds pretty accurate. Sometimes I wonder if I'll feel anything except nothing and pain ever again."

Quinn's understanding smile was answer enough.

"But you're wrong about one thing." She lifted her head from the headboard and met his intent gaze. "I still want to know why you have such a personal vendetta against Jackson Pepper."

His jaw worked as he looked away and stalled.

"The truth, Quinn," came her barely audible prod.

When he looked up, she recoiled from his eyes.

"Because he killed my wife."

Five

Kerstin gasped, not so much from surprise—she'd been ready for something monumental—but from the pain etched into his face, a pain that looked as though it would never go away. With what she knew about Pepper, and what she was learning about Quinn, she should have put two and two together. He'd even told her his wife was dead, and she'd seen the hollowness in him that first day they'd talked. She'd just missed the signs.

She fought an overwhelming urge to go to him, to comfort him, to take away the agony in his eyes. She would swear the words had tumbled out before he could stop them, just as she was sure he'd meant to tell her something else. But this was the truth. The raw, unvarnished, open-wound truth.

She had to clear her throat to get a squeak out before she said, "Somehow I have the feeling you're not trying to get him to the police."

Quinn shook his head. "He had his day in court. Justice failed."

"Can I ask what happened, or is it too painful to talk about?"

"I got in Pepper's way a few years ago. He paid me back by stabbing my wife. I'd been out of town. She'd been lying there for two days when I found her."

Kerstin closed her eyes against the onslaught of sadness pouring over her. Her decision to ask what happened had been one of those hellish choices—the need to know every possible detail for Meghan's sake, and the desire to hide her head in the sand. She'd chosen knowledge over the lure of blissful ignorance, and now her vivid imagination was making her pay.

"I'm sorry," he said as though from a mile away. "I shouldn't have told you."

"I asked. Thank you for not protecting me."

His laugh was a travesty of humor. "That's just it. It was my job to protect her. I failed."

Kerstin looked at his bowed head and for an instant saw her father. He felt that way about her mother's battle with Alzheimer's disease, as if he had done something wrong and the disease was his fault. Quinn so obviously had the same I'm-the-man-of-the-house syndrome she wasn't sure if she wanted to laugh or cry.

She couldn't think about her parents. She had to stay on track.

"And when you find him?" she asked, suspecting his answer, but forcing him to say the words.

"I'm going to kill him."

His shoulders stiffened. He obviously expected another gasp from her, maybe umbrage. Or fear. She didn't oblige him, though.

"You can't do that."

"Says who?"

"Says God."

"And just when did the Big Guy die and make you my conscience?"

"I'm not asking to be. I'm just answering your question."

Quinn threw himself backward into the bed, controlling the urge to slam his fist through the wall. Instead he turned off the light and listened as Kerstin settled in her bed.

It took a long, long time before he could speak again.

"What? No recriminations? No avowals to stop me?"

She didn't honor his sarcasm with a response in kind. Instead her voice came to him from the darkness, and he heard no hesitation, no uncertainty.

"Right now, I don't care what you have planned. You're driven to locate Pepper and that suits my needs. I'll deal with the rest when it happens.'' He heard her shift, her legs rustling against the sheets. ''Despite my big words, there have been moments I've wished him dead. Maybe I'll help you, who knows?''

He didn't believe her for a second. She didn't have the rage necessary to take the law into her own hands. But he did.

He'd also had as much emotional upheaval as he could handle for one day.

''Good night, Kerstin.''

''Sweet dreams, Quinn.''

He didn't hurt her feelings by laughing out loud. She obviously wasn't aware that hell hadn't frozen over yet.

When they arrived at the park the next morning— actually, it was a huge, privately owned field—Quinn pointed out Cindy and Jim, and Kerstin headed for their group. He left her, saying he was going to do some scouting and would meet her there in a while.

Their conversation had been minimal when they'd awakened, both of them needing time to digest their restless night and revelatory dialogue. She didn't want to admit it, but she was relieved to be away from him. She needed time to think.

So much had happened, and once again she felt she'd lost her balance. She fought against a building concern for Quinn and what he'd been through, and a sense of betrayal for allowing her focus to slip. No matter how much she empathized with Quinn's pain, his sense of injustice, his need for revenge, nothing was more important than getting Meghan out of harm's way. She hurt for him, more than she wanted to, but first things came first.

She simply could not let his soulful eyes and mouthwatering body affect her pulse anymore. That whiteout thing he'd talked about was amazingly accurate, and she had to stay numb—especially to Quinn. The last thing she needed was a sexual awakening in the midst of all this commotion.

Kerstin gave her head a clearing shake, feeling as if she were lost in a sea of leather and tattoos. And if it wasn't black leather and silver studs, it was black denim and black T-shirts. There were Harley-Davidson transfers, patches, banners, jackets, bandannas, koozies, watches and cigarettes. Kerstin had to give the company credit. They were marketing geniuses.

Kerstin stopped as a wave of despair washed over her. Everywhere were people who seemed to have dressed out of the same closet. How was she ever going to find Meghan in this mass of human lookalikes?

She made herself start walking again. It was her only option besides crumbling into a ball and bursting into tears, and she was grateful she wasn't the type to cry in public.

Kerstin looked around her and wondered how things had come to this. Her fun-loving, sometimes hopelessly irresponsible sister was in danger. Now she was playing concerned-sister-cum-private-detective, and had dealt into a hand where the stakes were life-and-death. Kerstin's most daring act before this ordeal had been to sink some of her hard-earned money into a high-risk stock.

All Meghan's messes to date had been innocent, easily rectified with the payment of a fine, or arrangements on a late bill. Kerstin loved her sister and knew it was going to take a little more time than average for Meghan to grow up. It was sadly ironic that Meghan had been making great strides in getting her life in order when Pepper had entered the picture.

Kerstin remembered well meeting the man. And Quinn was right—Pepper did have charm. He was in his forties, his blond hair stylishly cut, his physique trim. He looked every inch what he had claimed to be, but they all had found out too late that he'd never seen the far side of a real-estate license. He was a wheeler-dealer, all right. Just not in houses and land.

Kerstin hated to think it, but she couldn't blame Meghan for falling for him. Her own pulse had sped up a little at Pepper's good looks and easy charisma, but her stomach had also knotted and now she knew why. Her instincts had been warning her about the man, but she'd made the classic fool's mistake—being deceived by beauty. She felt like an idiot for being so gullible.

The question still remained, however, of whether Meghan could be saved from the clutches of this particular snake. And Kerstin refused to give up. While there were still questions, there was hope. And she didn't want to admit it, but her heart believed Quinn was going to be the key.

Kerstin reacquainted herself with Cindy and took the seat offered to her by Jim on the bench. She gratefully accepted a cup of hot, steaming coffee and took a careful sip. She let the conversation float around her as she waited for Quinn to join them, planning to speak up if an opportunity presented itself, but for now, she was content to listen to the banter between these obviously longtime friends.

Her thoughts drifted back to last night and her discussion with Quinn. He hadn't believed her about helping him kill Pepper. And maybe she couldn't, but that didn't matter.

What mattered was sticking closer to Quinn than ever, knowing what she knew now. If he did intend to kill Pepper—and she couldn't really say she blamed him no matter what she was "supposed" to feel—she had to make sure Meghan was out of harm's way when Quinn made his move.

Quinn tossed the beer he'd been offered into a trash can as he headed back to Kerstin. He'd pretended to drink as he'd chatted with some old acquaintances, all the while hoping he didn't run into Benji or any of his pals. There was always a risk someone would recognize him as he'd been a bike fan for years, but for now he believed his profession was still a secret.

Otherwise, he'd be paralyzed with fear of getting a knife between his ribs. He couldn't work that way. Besides, his internal radar was pretty quiet, so he was as comfortable as he could be.

The morning had passed quickly, and he was as hopeful as he'd been in months. He didn't want to overreact, but if what he'd heard as he'd made the rounds of the rougher campsites was true, he was close to his quarry. The frustrating part was no one knew exactly when Pepper was supposed to show.

Quinn's logistical dilemma increased as he made his way across the park. He couldn't be in two places at once, and he didn't want Kerstin near the hardened, more crude groups he'd been chatting with. He didn't want her out of his sight the whole day, either. So, how could he watch for Pepper and protect Kerstin at the same time? He'd rather the stubborn minx had stayed at the motel, but he knew there was no chance of that happening.

"Hey, sexy!"

Cindy's foghorn voice cut through his musings and made him realize he had reached his destination.

Surely that flash of irritation on Kerstin's face wasn't jealousy? Moments like this made it hard to keep his emotions away from the woman who stole into his thoughts with frustrating regularity. His bruised and battered confidence might need to believe his lovely, naive companion wasn't immune to him, but he was determined to battle the attraction. He had one job and one job only—killing Jackson Pepper.

He didn't have any time or feelings to spare, and the last thing he needed was to have his soul awakened at this last moment.

No, it was fine to think of Kerstin as one incongruously hot, innocent little package, as long as he kept his hands off and his mind occupied elsewhere.

"Earth to Irish, come in, Irish."

Quinn smiled at Cindy. "Sorry, lost in thought."

"No duh," she teased, punching him in the arm.

He glanced at Kerstin, who was rolling her beautiful green eyes at Cindy's obvious flirtation. It didn't seem to faze Jim, though, who gave him a welcoming nod and returned his attention to the conversation at his end of the table.

Cindy vacated the place next to Kerstin, and Quinn sat down.

"Good morning," he said, putting a hand on her shoulder for a brief greeting. He hated the strain smudging her eyes and wished more than ever that this was all over.

"What's left of it anyway," Kerstin responded tartly. "What did you find out?"

He withdrew his hand, a grin tugging at his mouth. So much for worrying.

"I've heard Pepper's supposed to show up sometime today, so I'll need to hang out on the other side most of the time. Why don't you—"

"I'm coming with you."

"It's not a good—"

"I said I'm coming with you. If you try and lose me, I'll just show up over there anyway, so don't.''

The same acid-causing fear he'd felt when she'd threatened to hitchhike came back, only double. Things would probably be safe enough during the day. Everyone would be busy visiting, and attending the concert later in the evening. But once it was dark, and the amount of…imbibing…increased on the opposite side of the park… He didn't want to think about it. This was one situation where there was safety in numbers, and he needed Kerstin to stay with Jim and Cindy. She'd be fine with their group.

"Listen to me, Kerstin—"

She swung her face around, and with the way they were sitting, it put her beautiful nose quite close to his.

"No, you listen, Quinn. I know you're trying to protect me, but I've already got enough guilt about letting my priorities slip as it is.''

She paused, taking a deep breath.

"I promise not to be stupid, Quinn. I know I'm out of my element, but you're watching for Pepper and I'm watching for Meghan. You can't be in two places at one time, and you can't watch for two things at once.''

"Don't worry—"

"Don't worry? Are you crazy? Tell me the truth— if you find Pepper and Meghan, who are you going to go after?''

He only hesitated an instant, but it was too long.

"My point exactly," she said with a hard edge to her eyes. "You have your agenda and I have mine."

"Can I finish an entire sentence now?" he asked, knowing his voice betrayed his building anger.

She had the grace to look sheepish. "I'm—"

"Don't apologize. I'm just asking you to look at this from my perspective. I know you're anxious and worried, but the guys I'm hanging around aren't average Joes like Jim and Cindy. These are the kind of people who give bikers the stereotyped image—and they deserve it. They don't respect women, and they won't treat you nicely."

"I understand that."

"Then do you understand you won't be doing Meghan any favors if you're in the hospital with a knife wound or recovering from an assault?"

Why wouldn't the woman listen to him? She was making him crazy! An image of Haley's vacant eyes and colorless face flashed across his mind, and suddenly the picture became Kerstin, covered in blood. He wouldn't survive another nightmare like that, and he had to make her understand.

"Kerstin, if I promise to come get you if I see Meghan, will you stay with Jim and Cindy? Please, I'm not asking this lightly."

"Quinn, I—"

Risking everything, he let his fear show in his eyes. "I couldn't handle it if you got hurt, Kerstin."

He watched Kerstin battle herself, struggling with

her escalating need to find her sister and her common sense.

"I understand—"

"No, you don't. You've never seen a dead body, Kerstin. I have." He held her shoulders in his hands to let her feel his urgency. "This isn't a game."

"If you're trying to scare me, you're succeeding."

"Good."

"Even so, I'm not going to let my fear keep me from doing what I have to do."

"Will you promise to stay on this side of the park, then? I give you my word I'll check in with you and keep you updated."

She took a breath, and finally said, "So the plan is that if you find Meghan, you'll come get me and we'll figure out a way to get her away from Pepper? I understand this will all depend on where she is and a hundred other details we can't prepare for, but you won't act without me?"

"I promise."

"All right then. I'll stay out of trouble."

One of the smaller concerts was in full swing that evening, the crowd growing as more people arrived for the Friday night opening. The rally would last all weekend, a nonstop festival of music, food, mixing and mingling. Laughter abounded, but Kerstin found reason to curse her cooperative nature. Her nerves were on full-scale alert, and she was regretting her decision to let Quinn go off by himself.

In the harsh glare of the stage lights and the peripheral bright spots of lanterns, she was almost sure she saw Meghan. She didn't stop to think, taking off across the crowd of spectators while desperately trying to catch another glimpse of the woman who'd caught her eye.

She muttered a string of invectives at herself for possibly missing the first real chance she'd had to find Meghan since this whole nightmare began, and then at Quinn for influencing her. If he were there, his height alone would be helpful in searching the crowd.

She was winded by the time she finally gave up, and found herself at the far reaches of the park. As she looked around, Kerstin realized just what she'd done. Exactly as Quinn had been afraid, she was now lost among the fringe element that couldn't be avoided in a rally of this size. The adrenaline that had had her running across the grass and jumping over outstretched legs was now deserting her.

In its place was a petrifying fear. She tried to avoid looking directly at the people talking too loud and drinking too heavily. The men looked mean; nothing at all like Jim and his buddies. And the women looked hard—not friendly, if a little coarse, like Cindy.

She quickened her pace and headed back toward the lights of the concert stage—which suddenly seemed very far away. She'd almost made it to the invisible line of safety when she was grabbed from behind by a pair of beefy arms. The smell of whiskey

Get up to four **FREE** books, plus TWO bonus gifts! When you play...

The
LUCKY
STARS
GAME

HOW TO PLAY:

★ Carefully scratch away the silver circle. Then match the star sign revealed to those opposite to find out how many gifts we have for you!

★ When you send back the card you will receive specially selected Silhouette Desire® novels. These books have a cover price of at least £2.70 each, but they are yours to keep absolutely free.

★ There's no catch. You're under no obligation to buy anything. We charge you nothing for you're first shipment. And you don't have to make any minimum number of purchases.

★ The fact is thousands of readers enjoy receiving books through the post from the Reader Service™. They like the convenience of home delivery... they like getting the best new novels before they're available in the shops... and they love their subscriber Newsletter, featuring author news, horoscopes, competitions and much more!

★ We hope that you'll want to remain a subscriber. But the choice is yours – to continue or cancel, anytime at all. So why not take up our invitation, with no risk of any kind. You'll be glad you did!

NO COST! NO RISK! NO OBLIGATION TO BUY!

POST TODAY! NO STAMP NEEDED!

If offer card is missing, write to: The Reader Service, P.O. Box 236, Croydon, CR9 3RU

─ Y O U R S   F R E E ─

You'll also receive this stunning Starfish Necklace. Crafted with a lovely goldtone finish, this beautiful pendant is set with a sparkling crystal and hangs on a delicate chain. It's a lovely piece to add to your jewellery collection – *we're sure you'll love it.*

PLAY THE

LUCKY STARS

GAME

Just scratch away the circle with a coin. Then look for the matching star sign to see how many gifts you'll get!

WORTH 4 FREE BOOKS
PLUS
A NECKLACE *AND*
A SURPRISE GIFT

WORTH 4 FREE BOOKS
PLUS
A NECKLACE

WORTH 3
FREE BOOKS

WORTH 2
FREE BOOKS

YES! I have scratched away the silver circle. Please send me all the FREE gifts for which I qualify. I understand I am under no obligation to purchase any books, as explained on the back and on the opposite page. *I am over 18 years of age.*

D9HI

Surname (Mrs/Ms/Miss/Mr) _____ Initials _____
BLOCK CAPITALS PLEASE

Address _____

_____

_____ Postcode _____

Offer valid in the UK only and not available to current Reader Service subscribers to this series. Overseas and Eire please write for details. We reserve the right to refuse an application and applicants must be aged 18 years or over. Only one application per household. Offer expires 29th February, 2000. Terms and prices subject to change without notice.

As a result of this application you may receive further offers from Harlequin Mills & Boon and other reputable companies. If you do not want to share in this opportunity, please write to the Data Manager at the address overleaf.

Silhouette Desire is a registered trademark, used under license.

Accepting the free books places you under no obligation to buy anything. You may keep the books and gift and return the despatch note marked "cancel". If we don't hear from you, about a month later we will send you 6 brand new books and invoice postage and packing. You may cancel at any time, otherwise every month we'll send you 6 more books, which you may either purchase or return – the choice is yours.

*Terms and prices subject to change without notice.

---------- ◆ DETACH AND POST CARD TODAY. NO STAMP NEEDED! ◆ ----------

The Reader Service ™

FREEPOST CN81

Croydon

Surrey

CR9 3WZ

NO
STAMP
NEEDED

nearly gagged her as a man of indeterminate age and excess body hair turned her around.

"Where you goin' so fast, little mama?" he said as he undressed her with his eyes. His fingers roamed down to cup her bottom. "Come join the—" *burp* "—party. Me and Neil are a lot of fun, ain't we, Neil?"

"Tha'z right, Weaver."

Kerstin worked to keep her stomach from heaving and tried to straight-arm some distance between the offensive man and his breath, but she was no match for the muscles straining the sleeves of Weaver's T-shirt. She managed to shift her behind away from his kneading fingers, and tried for a smile. She was pretty sure she failed miserably.

"Thanks, um, but I've got to get back—"

"No, you don't," he argued, plunking her down on the seat of his motorcycle as if she weighed no more than his helmet. Neil, also of questionable parentage and sanitary practices, moved to block her in. She tried to calm her pulse and think, although she doubted reasoning with a drunk would accomplish much.

"Listen, guys," she said, knocking away the hand reaching for the zipper of her vest. She tried to dismount the bike. "I appreciate the offer, but really, I've got to—"

"Let the lady go, fellas."

Kerstin nearly cried out in relief at the sound of Quinn's voice. She was shaking so badly she was afraid her legs would fold underneath her, but she got off the motorcycle anyway. Her retreat toward Quinn was cut short by her unwanted host.

"This ain't your business, jack."

"The lady is my business and get your hands off her."

"You mean these?" Weaver asked as he spread one hand across her stomach to pull her back against him while the other hand latched onto her bare thigh. She could no longer see Weaver's face, but she imagined the light of challenge in Neil's eyes was reflected in his bloodshot depths, as well.

She stood perfectly still, somehow sure any movement on her part would provoke not only Weaver, but Quinn. Their voices drew the attention of the people nearby, and Kerstin began praying as she'd never prayed before.

The conversation around them began to taper off, and Kerstin felt sweat forming on her lip and brow. Quinn looked cool and mean, his face a sculpture of ice, and she realized she was now thoroughly scared. She wasn't just scared of Weaver and his wandering fingers, or his friend Neil—she was afraid of Quinn. Any lingering doubts about his ability to commit violence were completely dispelled.

"If you don't let her go—"

Weaver laughed, but a waver betrayed his fear. "You'll what? Kill me?"

Quinn's shrug was almost casual. "If you're lucky."

His voice was soft, perfectly calm. Kerstin had to believe she wasn't the only one who saw absolute determination in Quinn's eyes. She wasn't even the one being threatened, and she was so scared she was about to throw up. He was obviously unimpressed by the people gathering closer, and even someone as stupid as Weaver had to know no matter what happened, he wouldn't be around to see any retaliation against Quinn.

Neil's eyes betrayed his fear, although he pretended to be unimpressed. Weaver's grip loosened just enough to allow Kerstin to step out of his hold. She hurried across the few feet to Quinn's side, but knew instinctively not to touch him.

The tension was almost unbearable when a gravelly voice came from behind Quinn.

"Hey, Irish. Something wrong?"

The crowd parted and a man who looked reminiscent of Daddy in height and temperament stepped up next to Quinn.

"No, Sonny," Quinn said, his voice as hard as his eyes, "I don't think we have a problem."

A glance over her shoulder explained why the crowd behind Weaver and Neil began to slip away. A group of men who looked as though they ate oil pans for breakfast were forming a rough semicircle behind Quinn and Sonny.

"I didn't think so," Sonny said, his smile not reaching his eyes. Unlike Daddy, he was pure muscle and roughly handsome. "I'm figuring Weaver here didn't know this was your old lady. Am I right, Weaver?''

"Yeah, that's…that's right. I was just teasin' is all.''

Quinn drilled Weaver once more before he turned and walked away. Quinn didn't even look as he reached back and grabbed her arm, practically dragging her with him.

The crowd dispersed into smaller groups, and while Kerstin was fairly sure the danger had passed, she would rather have faced a charging bull than say anything to Quinn.

"What the hell was that all about?'' Sonny asked as they neared his campsite.

She flinched as Quinn's hand tightened on her arm for a second.

"Nothing I can't handle. Thanks for the backup, though.''

"No problem. Weaver's just a moron when he's sober, but he's unpredictable when he's drunk. I wouldn't let him and his kind catch you alone, if you know what I mean.''

Quinn nodded. Sonny thrust out his wrist, and Kerstin was sure a message passed between the two men as they shook hands. She didn't have time to analyze the moment before she was pinned by Sonny's gaze. It was odd, but he reminded her so much of Quinn it made her stomach clench, although the two men looked nothing alike. Sonny flicked a glance back to Quinn and then walked away.

Kerstin had to practically dig her heels into the ground to get Quinn to stop. As it was, he'd run her halfway across the park and she was out of breath.

"Just a minute, Quinn."

He didn't say one word. He let her catch some air and then towed her the rest of the way to his bike. She was smart enough to stay silent during the ride back to the hotel.

He allowed her to precede him into the room, and she winced when he slammed the door. She knew she should be angry and feisty, standing up to him for his barbaric behavior, but her legs were trembling as the last half hour replayed itself in her mind. And she couldn't sort out how much of her should be resentful of his high-handedness and how much should be grateful to him for saving her neck. For the first time in her life, she was afraid she was going to faint.

She sat down on her bed before her legs gave out.

Quinn went into the bathroom and shut the door, leaving her in an oppressive silence broken only by the sound of water running in the sink and a splashing noise she assumed meant he was dousing his face in cold water.

She was sitting in exactly the same spot a few moments later when he came out. He just stood there, staring at her. Then he took her by the shoulders and hauled her to her feet.

Six

"**D**amn it, woman," he ground out, his eyes boring into hers. "Don't you know what could have happened to you out there?"

She didn't have time to think, much less answer, before he pulled her against his chest and his mouth descended on hers in a powerful kiss.

It wasn't painful or punishing. An oddly detached portion of her brain characterized it as a little desperate before all rational thought fled.

The only thing she could concentrate on was the feel of his body against the length of hers. One strong arm weighted her back, pressing her breasts into the solid wall of his chest. The other arm was slung around her waist, his hand splayed on her hip, keeping her thighs locked with his.

A moan was wrenched from deep inside her as he slanted his mouth the other direction and he teased her with a gentle brush of his lips against the kiss-swollen fullness of hers. He took advantage of her gasp to delve inside and beckon her with velvet strokes of his tongue.

She wasn't even aware she'd flung her arms around his neck until she realized she was tunneling her fingers into the soft strands of his dark hair, begging with her hands and her whimpers for more.

She didn't protest when he took a step backward and they fell onto the bed. Nothing could have made her move from the warmth and safety of his arms. A thought tried to slip in that she was being foolish, that she wouldn't be acting this way if she weren't distraught, but she ruthlessly quelled it. Truth or not, she didn't care.

Quinn's assault of lips and tongue became a rain of gentle touches against her eyes, her nose, her cheeks, her chin. His strong white teeth nibbled at her ear and made a path down the side of her neck where he stopped to suck at the hollow of her throat. She protested when he shifted his weight, but caught her breath when she felt the slide of her zipper being pulled down.

The cool air raised goose bumps on her flesh now barely hidden by her scant black bra. It seemed to disappear into thin air, but she gave it no further thought as Quinn's hot breath on the curve of her breast claimed all her attention. She nearly screamed in frustration as she waited for him to take her aching nipple into his mouth, the sound coming out as a high-pitched moan when she felt his tongue touch the hardened tip. Her hips came off the bed, her body surging against the sensation. He spread one hand across her buttocks and anchored her to him as he took her fullness into his mouth.

She heard herself whispering, "Please, please," but she didn't know what she was asking for. She'd never experienced anything like this, never known a passion so overwhelming. Her limited experience had never even hinted at something so marvelous. Her skin had never tingled as if too sensitive to touch, yet knowing she would die if he stopped. Her body had never cried out with such pure, sexual need.

He leaned back long enough to yank his shirt off and she couldn't get enough of the feel of the crisp hairs on his chest against her breasts. She memorized the muscles of his shoulders and arms by touch, her strokes turning into claw marks as his fingers slid up between her thighs and his hand cupped her most intimate place.

Instinct let her help him get the rest of her clothes off. She wanted to tell him to hurry, to beg him to touch her again, but the words came out as whimpers and her hands trembled as she clutched his chest. When he found her slick warmth, she cried out, arching her back in a mindless attempt to get closer and yet retreat from the onslaught against her senses.

His mouth took possession of hers as he found her

center, his callused fingers against that sensitive nub making her mindless with need. It took a mere moment for the torrent to build, sweeping her up into a place of unbearable pleasure. And then her world exploded and he caught her sob against his lips.

She had no idea how long he caressed her with the gentlest of touches, how many kisses he placed on her shoulders, her breasts, her stomach, before she returned to her body from the heaven she'd flown to. All she knew was he was now as naked as she and her fingers at last could caress his buttocks, his spine, his thighs.

The tide was building once more under his expert tutelage. She wanted him so badly, she heard herself saying again, "Please, please," but he didn't move between her beckoning thighs. She wanted to weep, then forgot why as his mouth trailed fire from her collarbone to her navel and below.

When his mouth covered where his fingers had just been, she knew with certainty that she was going to die. His hands caught her hips, not allowing any escape from the indescribable experience. Long slow sweeps of heat made her eyes roll back into her head. When he pinpointed his attack with quick flicks of the tip of his tongue, she was powerless to stop the cascade as she crested heaven again.

When she could gasp enough air to keep from fainting, she caught his long soft hair in her hands and yanked his head back. This time she didn't beg. She demanded.

''Now.''

His smile was thoroughly male, and would have been thoroughly irritating if she hadn't been sure she couldn't stand another second without him. Her hands clenched into the sheets as he covered her.

Quinn watched her eyes grow wide as he finally sheathed himself inside her softness. He loved the sound escaping from her, a combination of a sigh and a groan. She wrapped her legs around his and tightened her muscles to keep him there, but he needed no urging to hold on to this moment. If his face looked anything like hers, she was experiencing a sense of fullness, of completion, just as he was.

When he began to move, he reveled in watching her, listening to the noises she made, feeling her fingernails mark him as she could not control her responses. Her body met his every stroke, so open, so giving. He wrapped his arms around her as need demanded the pace. She threaded her fingers through his hair and held on, fusing her mouth to his as she strained against him, finding her release once more. Her orgasm made her tighten around him, demanding he come with her. He complied, crushing her against him as he cried out against her throat.

She didn't seem to mind the inability to breathe as he continued to hold her. He concentrated on the nipping kisses she was applying to his neck. He tried to move from her, but she kept her legs locked with his, refusing to relinquish the joining.

Light-headedness finally weakened her grasp, and

he rolled onto his side, taking her with him, but relieving her of his weight. He was struggling to breathe just as hard as she was, but he made sure his hands left no doubt that he wanted her close. His heart pounded madly in his chest and his muscles were still quivering.

He held her to his heart until his arms went numb, then reluctantly, he rolled out of bed and tugged her into a sitting position.

"Come on. Let's get a shower."

"Quinn—"

He placed his finger against her mouth. "No. No talking. No rationalizing. No listing why we shouldn't have done that and how we'll regret it. There's time for that tomorrow."

She looked for a moment as though she'd argue, but she finally shut her beautiful, kiss-swollen lips and gave him a tenuous smile.

With the spray on full and the water the perfect balance between too hot and too cold, he took his precious time working shampoo through her hair, inhaling the warm, citrusy scent and enjoying sliding his fingertips against her head. It was just as much fun to rinse out the mountain of bubbles, getting his fill of playing with her silken tresses until they were squeaky-clean.

He lathered a washrag while Kerstin stood with her face tipped back into the spray, then rolled her head forward to let the water pound her neck. She tried to help as he began washing her arms and neck, but he patiently removed her hands and told her without words to put them behind the showerhead and leave them there. She closed her eyes, but that was okay with him. He was getting too much enjoyment out of watching his hands make a soapy trail over her skin, from her delicate shoulders, over her beautiful breasts, down her flat stomach and over the flare of her hips. He was especially gentle as he washed the sweat and sex from between her legs, hoping he hadn't made her sore. He'd tried to be gentle, tried to take his time, but she'd made him so hot he was afraid he'd had about as much finesse as a schoolboy.

His body was reacting again, with an almost painful intensity. He tried to think of something else, but it was difficult with his hands slipping around her luscious thighs.

He turned her around, but that didn't do any good. Now he was distracted by the sway of her spine. No wonder painters since the dawn of time have tried to capture the sensuality of a woman's back narrowing to a tiny waist. Kerstin's flared into buttocks so beautiful he couldn't keep his hands off.

It finally struck his befuddled brain that Kerstin was holding her breath. He looked up to find her clutching the shower post as if she could hardly stand.

He hadn't intended to seduce her in the shower. He'd wanted her to stay in the wonderful world of forgetfulness a little while longer and his plan had been to wash her gently, dry her softly and put her to bed and let her sleep.

When she turned around, her face was anything but sleepy and he knew his plan was a failure. Somehow, by the look in her eyes, he had the feeling he wasn't going to mind.

Kerstin took the rag from Quinn's hand and tried to contain the maelstrom he had so easily rebuilt inside her. She wanted him to press her against the tile and drive into her with mindless need. But even more, she needed to touch him, to do to him what he'd done to her. Did he know? Did he have a clue that she would go insane if he didn't take her again and make her go to that place she'd never been before?

She struggled with her breathing as she made him assume the position he'd put her in. Her fingers trembled as she used the cloth to trace the contours of his chest. His nipples were hard, as hard as hers, and she let the water wash away the soap before she took his little pebble in her mouth. It was gratifying to hear him struggle to breathe, to feel the muscles in his arms quiver as he held them over his head.

He was hard, demanding, as she used bubbles to lubricate her hands and make her fingers slip around him in a torturous rhythm.

She waited until she knew she'd driven him just to the edge before she let him go, slowly lathering his hard-muscled thighs with the talent of a temptress. She had no idea where she'd learned to be such a tease. Heaven knew she'd never been anywhere near as abandoned as she was being with Quinn.

It was easier not to think about it. It was much

more fun to rinse off his body and kneel down to let her mouth do the teasing now, slipping her tongue up the length of him, feeling his thighs clench under her massaging fingers. She'd never had the desire to taste a man before, but with instinct, if not much skill, she could tell she was driving him insane.

She laughed, a delighted, husky sound when he pulled her to her feet and thrust her against the tile wall. She was too busy battling tongues with him to notice the cold, only moaning into his mouth in invitation when he pulled her knee up to wrap her leg around his. He thrust into her with a most satisfying urgency and she arched her head back as he drove into her and gave her exactly what she wanted.

She was glad she came back to earth in time to open her eyes and watch him take his pleasure, his cry harsh against her ear but sounding more beautiful than any music.

He kept her trapped but pressed his head against the tile beside her. "Damn it, woman—"

"You said that before." She used her fingernails to trace a path in the drops of water on his back.

He lifted his head and looked at her in confusion. "What?"

"Before we made love the first time. You said, 'damn it, woman,' just like you did now."

He caught her chin in a gentle grip and matched his forehead to hers. "That's because you're making me crazy."

She smiled. She couldn't help it. If he had meant

to intimidate her or make her contrite, he failed miserably.

"Don't expect me to apologize," she said as he put her back under the shower spray. This time he allowed no nonsense as he washed her.

His hand paused on her back. "If you do, I'll spank you."

She was sure a good, solid feminist such as herself shouldn't admit the delightful shiver his mock threat gave her.

He made her behave as he gave himself a quick once-over with the soap and rinsed off. He turned off the taps and thrust open the curtain.

She couldn't help it. When he stretched to grab the towels, she reached over and tweaked his nipple.

"Damn—"

"It, woman," she said for him, in a voice as low as she could make it. The effect was spoiled by a giggle.

He merely grunted and threw a towel at her, wrapping his own around his lean hips as he stepped out. By the time she'd rubbed most of the excess water from her hair and joined him in the other room, he was dried, had combed his hair and was safely hidden between the sheets.

Hidden from the waist down, anyway, she amended with disappointment. She felt awkward for the first time as she slipped on a pair of underwear and found her sleep shirt. Flipping her damp hair out her face, she noticed that he had scooted over to the wall and was holding the corner of the blankets down invitingly.

She paused.

"Come on, Kerstin. Your bed is all sweaty. Let's use mine."

It was silly to be self-conscious now, she told herself. Not after all that had happened.

She tried for nonchalant as she grabbed the pillows from her bed and moved next to him. She sat down to slide under the covers, shivering as the crisp hairs on his legs scraped deliciously along her calves.

He waited until she was settled and shifted onto his side, propping his head up with his hand. The sudden quiet and his blue-eyed scrutiny were a tiny bit unnerving.

"You know," he said, making her jump.

She waited for him to finish, trying to look more confident than she felt.

"No, what?" she finally asked.

"You surprised me."

She felt her entire body flame in an extended blush. It didn't matter that he couldn't see under the covers. She still felt her toes heating up.

"I surprised me, too," she muttered.

"I guess I couldn't imagine you being so... unreserved."

He smiled, darn his soul, enjoying her discomfort. Maybe she deserved it for that tweak....

"Blame it on six solid weeks of relentless tension and anxiety."

"Don't get me wrong," he assured her, dimples appearing in his cheeks in an alarmingly attractive way. "I'm not complaining. Not by a long shot."

Kerstin wondered if it were truly possible for someone to spontaneously combust, because that's exactly what she felt was going to happen if he kept teasing her in his deep, drawling voice.

"Well," she cleared her throat, "let's just say I'm acting a little outside my norm these days."

His smile disappeared and his fingers were oh-so-gentle as he pulled her chin up so she'd look at him again. "Then don't go back to normal, Kerstin."

Tears sprang to her eyes, surprising and embarrassing her at the same time. "Why do you have to be so nice?" she whispered, clenching her eyelids to keep the tears from escaping.

"What do you mean?" he asked quietly, unsettling her even more by brushing the hair back from her forehead with whisper softness.

"Nothing," she lied, groping for some explanation that didn't sound moronic. How could she tell him he was the kind of man she'd dreamed about, a not-so-shiny knight who made her heart race and her soul fly? How could she even consider falling in love with a man who had no past, no future, and she barely knew his name?

He was still watching her.

"I...uh...I was just wishing there were more guys like you around, I guess. You're caring, sexy as all get-out, and despite our not-so-smooth start, you've been more honest with me than any guy I've ever known.''

A flash of something akin to pain made him wince. She was about to ask him what that meant when he leaned down and kissed her question out of her mind.

She was still foggy-headed when he reached over her to turn out the light. He curled around her, spoon-fashioned, and she was sure there was no better way imaginable to sleep. Rapidly losing the battle with exhaustion, she barely had time to say, ''Good night, Quinn,'' before her eyes fluttered shut.

Seven

Between cursing himself soundly and lecturing himself on being an idiot, Quinn's few dreams had been anything but sweet. For most of the night he'd watched her, aching with pleasure at what they'd shared, and with pain at what was to come.

His self-recriminations hadn't been enough to make him keep his hands off her, rolling her over to kiss her awake in the deep quiet of the night. They'd made love without haste, their earlier urgency satisfied. Her sighs had been soft, her pleasure a gradual building to a culmination leaving her replete. She'd watched his enjoyment of her body, still a touch of naiveté in her eyes that he could want her so badly. He'd taken his time to show her just how much pleasure she gave him before his own body had demanded release.

He'd held her close again while she'd returned to her dreams. All too soon, weak sunshine slipped under the curtains, bringing with it a full measure of agony. He watched her in the dim light, wondering how he could feel the most content he'd ever felt in his life, and at the same time like the biggest heel ever to walk the earth.

Her words of yesterday sang a haunting melody in his mind. *You've been more honest with me than any guy I've ever known.*

So, how did he tell her that not only had he been dishonest, he was more appropriately a bald-faced liar? How was there any hope of salvaging what they'd started last night? How could he tell her he was nothing like the man she imagined him to be, that he was a Texas Ranger, not a rogue biker? And even that wasn't the whole truth. He was a Ranger on paper only at the moment, and maybe not even on paper for long.

The point was, he couldn't tell her anything more than he'd already revealed, and he had nothing to offer her but misery. He was already a felon by his mere planning to commit murder. He was the worst kind of felon on top of that—a cop gone bad. His job was supposed to uphold the law, to be a purveyor of justice. He was a Texas Ranger, for heaven's sake.

He was a fraud.

She lay there so trustingly in his arms, snuggled against his side, and she didn't know he kept a gun in the holster attached to the inside of one boot and a knife in the other.

She didn't know he was about to break her heart.

Kerstin awoke to the sight of Quinn's blue eyes watching her. She had the impression he'd been doing that for a long time, but she felt too good to be embarrassed. She smiled and pulled his head down for a kiss, memorizing every second of his warm lips against hers, his callused fingers caressing her cheek, his heart beating against her breast.

Although not a complete innocent, she had never experienced anything this intimate before. She realized intimacy was so much more than just naked flesh pressed together. It was a connection between two people defying explanation.

She'd given him a part of her soul, and she wasn't sure she was completely comfortable with the knowledge. It was also something she needed time to come to terms with, but she'd deal with that later.

Slipping from the bed, she headed for the bathroom.

"I'm going to soak in the bathtub until my skin wrinkles up. Want to join me?"

Despite the flare of desire in his eyes, he shook his head. "Maybe in a little while. I have to make a couple of phone calls."

She tried not to let her disappointment show before she disappeared around the corner. She stepped into the tub, relaxing as hot water slowly rose around her and the roar of the tap filled the silence.

As the delightful soreness in her muscles began to ease, a plan formulated in her mind. She decided, since she was already acting so far outside her normal parameters, she might as well make as much use of her temporary insanity as she could. She didn't want to think this might be her last chance to experience the joy Quinn had given her, so she hurried to rinse her hair. Then she was ready to put her plot to lure Quinn into more soapy mischief into action.

She wrapped a towel around herself, careful to use the strategic gap to her best advantage, revealing a bit of upper thigh and naked hip. Opening the door quietly, she peeked around the corner and smiled to see Quinn's back turned toward her as he sat on the bed, facing the phone. She tiptoed closer, envisioning his surprise when she got close enough to nibble the back of his neck.

"Sonny Bickler, and he said Pepper would be here late today."

His voice stopped her in her tracks. She couldn't explain it, but he sounded different, not at all like the man she'd been spending nearly every waking moment with.

"Listen, man, don't do that. When I took off my star, it was my career I torpedoed. You're my partner, but you don't have… Yeah, well, thanks."

Kerstin stayed frozen.

"I hope not. Bickler says he won't arrest Meghan unless he has to. I—yeah, I've got the sister—''

Quinn suddenly whirled around, locking eyes with her. Something had obviously alerted him to her presence—maybe the mew of pain she couldn't quite keep silent.

"I gotta go," he said into the phone and hung up. He stood and faced her. "Kerstin—''

"You bastard," she whispered, clutching her towel around her wounded dignity. She was afraid if she loosened her grip, she'd go after his throat like an insane woman, her hands transformed into claws.

"Let me expl—''

"So, what are you? FBI? DEA?"

"Texas Ranger."

Kerstin sneered. "So, where's your white hat and tin star, Ranger?"

He didn't flinch at her sarcasm. "In Austin, on my desk." He rubbed a hand over his face. "Kerstin, I'm sorry—''

"Go to hell and rot." She grabbed her bag off the floor and stormed back into the bathroom, locking the door behind her.

She stood at the sink, clutching the cool counter. How had she gone from heaven to hell so quickly? How could her world crash in mere seconds?

The trembling started in her hands, traveling quickly until her whole body was shaking. She ignored the pounding on the door and finally gathered enough strength to step into the shower. It was probably absurd, but she kept the towel secured around her as she let cool water wash over her and bathe her heated face.

She had no idea how long she stood under the spray, but there wasn't enough water in the ocean to wash away the ache in her heart or the knot in her stomach. She could stand there a year and never feel warm again. Finally fatigue got the better of her and she had to get out. Trading her wet towel for a dry one, she twisted a second one around her hair to keep it off her rapidly chilling skin. She dried off with quick, rough strokes—just enough so she could dress.

She rummaged through her bag to get the warmest things she could find, which turned out to be a long-sleeved shirt and a pair of jeans, but with socks and shoes, and the light jacket waiting outside, she would be okay.

It was too much to hope for that he would be gone, so she took a fortifying breath and went out, avoiding Quinn by hunting down her shoes and putting them on.

"Finished?"

His tone betrayed nothing to her. After scraping enough courage together to look at him, she found his face revealed as little as his voice.

"Yes," she said, managing somehow to sound calm. She proved herself a fraud by nervously twitching the zipper of the jacket she'd slipped on.

"What do you want to know first?"

"I'm not sure what to ask," she replied as a cold

resolve stole into her, which at least stopped the trembling. "Or even if it matters what I ask because I'm not sure I can believe anything you've said or..."

She cut herself off, wishing she could snatch back the words.

"Done?" he finished for her, scooting to the edge of the bed until he sat across from her.

He didn't touch, but his hand reached out to her.

"Kerstin, if you believe nothing else, believe that last night was real, for me, anyway. More real than anything I've ever experienced."

Her throat constricted. "I don't want to talk about last night," she whispered hoarsely.

"All right, then let me see if I can take care of some of the obvious questions. I am a Texas Ranger. I was married to a woman named Haley. Jackson Pepper did kill her."

"Why?"

"Why did he kill her?" Quinn clarified.

She nodded.

"Before I became a Ranger, I was a trooper. I stopped Pepper on a routine speeding violation. He had white powder on his pants and the seat of his car, and no donut box in sight. Due to his erratic driving, I asked to search the vehicle. He refused, of course. I had sufficient probable cause so I put him in the patrol car and found a suitcase of white powder, neatly packaged, in the trunk."

"Don't tell me," she interrupted. "He beat it on illegal search and seizure."

"That's what his lawyer was going to try, but the indictment never went to trial because the dope went missing from the evidence room."

"So he walked."

"Scot-free…and smiled at me the whole time he promised I'd pay. He killed Haley two years later."

"You couldn't have known. You couldn't have stopped him."

He didn't argue with her. "Kerstin, I really do want to help you find Meghan," he said some moments later.

"So you can arrest her!"

"No—"

"I heard you."

"You heard me say that Sonny will only arrest her if he has to. If he feels she's been aiding or abetting—"

"Meghan would never do that—"

"I know you love your sister, Kerstin, but you have to look at this from the law's point of view."

"The hell I do! All I've cared about from day one is getting my sister away from a madman. She would never help someone like Pepper."

"And I believe you, but I'm not in charge of this case." He looked away. "I'm not in charge of any cases right now."

"Is Sonny a Ranger?"

"No, he's with the Bureau. I had no idea he was even here. He risked a lot by stepping up to help me—us. I'm sure I don't have to explain to you that his life, not to mention mine, is in your hands. They wouldn't be able to find enough pieces of his body to identify if anyone finds out Sonny's a lawman.''

"I'm not stupid, Quinn."

"I know. I just had to say it, for my conscience's sake. I've too many regrets as it is."

She couldn't stop a frown. "That argument might be more compelling if I felt you had a conscience."

He didn't so much as flinch. "I'm afraid I can't defend that point with you."

When she saw the hollowness in his eyes, she ruthlessly ignored the stab of pain in her heart. She would not feel compassion for him. She would not remember how much he'd lost. She would stay focused on Meghan no matter what.

"Don't worry about Sonny. His secret is absolutely safe with me. And yours is, too. You have to know I would never say anything that would hurt you…no matter how angry I am at the moment."

He nodded. "I know. Listen, Kerstin—"

"No," she said, cutting him off. "No more. Not right now. Let's just get going."

The trip to the grounds was uncomfortable, to say the least. Kerstin had no choice but to ride with him, and it churned her insides to be so close to him when her emotions were turned inside out.

They separated quickly. She had begrudgingly agreed to meet him every two hours at Jim and Cindy's table, knowing she couldn't let her hurt feelings cause a foolish mistake that could cost her her sister. Things were getting too hot.

Sheer force of will kept her mind blank as she scanned the crowd. For hours she walked, stopping to visit the few people she knew, then starting her trek all over again. Lunch came and went as a tasteless blur, but she ate to keep her energy up. She stayed around the food vendors the longest, figuring even Pepper had to eat sometime, and maybe, just maybe, Meghan would be with him.

She was so intent on her mission that she passed over the woman with auburn hair, and had to jerk her attention back.

It was Meghan!

Kerstin tried to casually blend in with a group watching an impromptu game of volleyball. The net was stretched between two trees, and the court had no exact markings, so she didn't feel too conspicuous.

Meghan was sitting in the middle of a big crowd of dangerous-looking men. Her face was strained, but she didn't seem overly frightened. Kerstin's stomach was tied in a knot from wondering what to do. She couldn't approach her sister—that would be the height of stupidity. But she didn't want to leave and get Quinn. What if Meghan wasn't there when she got back?

Kerstin was still chewing her thumbnail when Meghan's group stood almost in unison and began moving toward the music stage. She did her best to

follow, losing sight of Meghan only to breathe in relief when a glimpse of auburn hair relieved her panic.

But hope turned into a cry of anguish when the sea
of people parted again, revealing a redhead who was
definitely not Meghan. Kerstin had no idea who this
woman was, and realized she'd gotten mixed up as
the pack had woven its way through the milling
crowds.

She searched, frantic, trying to pick up Meghan's
trail again. She even climbed onto the table of some
very surprised bikers to try and catch a glimpse from
a better vantage point.

Her legs were shaking when she finally climbed
down, apologizing for interrupting so rudely. The
guys accepted with confused good grace, asking if
they could help.

She shook her head absently as she walked away,
her heart in despair.

So close. She'd been so close. Kerstin barely realized she'd made it to Jim's camp when she collapsed beneath a tree and hid her face in her hands.

Quinn almost didn't see her, but instinct had made
him look at the small form sitting at the base of the
tree, her head bent to her knees and her shoulders
shaking with sobs. His gut clenched so hard he felt
nauseated.

He rushed to her and crouched down, putting his
hand on her arm. "Kerstin? What's wrong?"

She lifted her face and his heart nearly broke. Her

cheeks were white, her eyes bright with unshed tears. It scared him more than anything else she could have done when she let him take her into his arms.

"I saw her, Quinn. I saw her and I lost her. Oh, God, she looked so horrible. I lost her yesterday, and I lost her again today. What am I going to do?"

He rocked her against him, stroking her hair as the sobs began again. "It's all right, sweetheart. I thought I had them, too, but they took off just as I got to the parking lot. My bike was too far away to follow. But I found out Pepper will definitely be back tomorrow. This time we'll be ready."

"What if I miss her? I don't think she can take much more."

Quinn didn't think Kerstin could take much more, either, but he didn't voice his fear. "We won't. I promise—we'll find Meghan tomorrow."

His low, vehement promise somehow calmed her, and her tears faded to jerking gasps. He didn't let her argue as he took her back to the hotel and urged her into a hot shower.

The sun hadn't even set yet when she came out in her nightshirt. He took her hand and pulled her onto his bed. He leaned against the wall and snuggled her against his chest. His legs framed her on either side, and she shifted until she was sideways and rested her head on his shoulder.

"I still hate you, you know," she said, scrubbing her cheek against his shirt.

"I know."

He didn't even consider telling her that he'd just been struck blindsided with the knowledge that he loved her. He was still in a bit of shock. It had overwhelmed him as he'd sat there, listening to the shower, and he'd realized he wasn't picturing her naked—although that was a pleasant thought—but rather, was worried about how he was going to soothe her troubled spirit.

What was more noteworthy, however, was the absolute calm with which he sat there, accepting the newfound revelation. Shouldn't he be denying this to himself for all he was worth? Shouldn't he be pacing frantically, or better yet, running for his life? Yet, here he sat, pressing kisses onto the smooth temple of the woman who'd stolen his heart.

He tucked her hair behind her ear and stroked her chin with a gentle rhythm of his thumb. Funny, it didn't even hurt to admit that he hadn't fallen for Haley this way. Theirs had been a slow, gradual building from friendship to marriage. Quinn decided he'd probably fallen head over heels for Kerstin the moment he'd set eyes on her—he'd just been too busy convincing himself his response was purely hormonal. As he recalled, he'd labeled it lust. And truth be told, there was a fair dose of that still in the mix.

"I wouldn't be talking to you if I wasn't so upset."

The softness of her voice belied her words. He smiled against the top of her head.

"I know, sweetheart."

"And don't call me sweetheart."

"Okay, honey."

He was well aware that the situation was entirely illogical. His world was topsy-turvy, his heart was just begging to be squashed—yet, here he sat, if not content, at least at peace for a while.

She'd never know he loved her. She didn't need to know, didn't need any more burdens on her too-slender shoulders. It was enough that he knew. He would be the keeper. It was his rightful sentence, after all—to know he loved her and that she could never feel the same way about him. He deserved a lifetime of living with that knowledge after hurting her so badly. And he could bear it—if he kept her safe, if he knew she returned to her old life with a minimum of scars. No matter what his choices in the next day or so, he would forever be denied access to her world—by his own decree. It would all be worth it, if he knew she was all right, if her world was restored to some semblance of sanity.

She deserved that knight she dreamed about. If anyone had earned a home and children and happiness, it was Kerstin. She gave so much, and didn't even realize how much of herself she so freely offered. He prayed she would find the man who could be her other half, the man who would make her smile.

His heart constricted with jealousy at the mere thought of another man holding her this way, but it had to be. It had to.

His eyes clenched shut when he felt her lips whisper against the side of his neck. He pretended for a moment it hadn't happened, that it was his imagination, because he could not, would not, take advantage of her. No matter how badly every nerve in his body screamed to pull her head back and plunder the sweet warmth of her mouth with his tongue, to use his hands and his lips to awaken the storm of passion he knew resided in her, he would not do it.

Then she kissed his throat. He could hardly breathe. His hands trembled from keeping his fingers clenched in a fist and away from the very skin he'd stroked comfortingly mere moments ago.

"Kerstin," he gasped. "Don't do that."

She didn't listen, stubborn female that she was.

"I mean it," he said, his voice faint. "You don't know what you're doing."

He felt her lips smile against his neck. He didn't know that was possible.

"Oh, yes, I do," she argued, shifting around so that she straddled his straight leg.

Grasping her arms, he held her back, desperately trying to hold on to his resolve. "No, you don't. You're hurt and you're scared. You don't want to do this."

"Deny you want me," she challenged.

His laugh was tortured. "I can't deny the painfully obvious, but I won't use you, Kerstin. No matter what you think of me, I'm not that big a bastard."

She shrugged his hands away and took hold of his shoulders, not flinching as she looked deeply into his eyes. "You have no idea what I think about you right now."

She wriggled closer on his thigh, and he bit his lip to keep silent.

"You're going to regret this in the morning."

Her smile said, "Silly man." "Of course I'm going to regret this in the morning. But it's not morning now, and that has nothing to do with it anyway."

"It should."

"Probably, but tonight I'm scared and lonely, and you're warm and strong."

"That's still pretty shaky reasoning."

"I don't want to be reasonable. I want to be held and kissed and touched. I want to know, just for a little while, that I'm not alone."

He sighed and struggled for control.

"I know you won't use me, Quinn, but I have every intention of using you. I know what I want." Her eyes dropped for the first time. "I need *you*, despite every logical argument. I need to pretend my world isn't falling apart, if just for tonight."

"But I can't risk hurting you, no matter how much you think you want this."

She put her hands on each side of his face. "Then be gentle."

That wasn't the kind of hurt he meant and she knew it, but she wasn't listening anymore. She was too busy sliding her fingers through his hair and planting tiny kisses on his eyes, his nose, his cheeks. As she ran her tongue down the side of his neck, he vowed he'd give her the release she needed, he'd even hold her all night long, but he would not give in to the desire already raging through him.

When she pulled far enough away to look at him again, he drank in the beauty of her face.

"I think I'm insulted," she said, her tone belying the hurt of her words. "You're being awfully pragmatic to a woman who's trying to seduce you."

Then she pressed the velvet softness of her lips against his, and he was lost. Wrapping his arms around her, he crushed her to him and kissed her with all the passion pent up inside him. All the rioting emotions focused into one thing—pleasing her. Fear became a conviction to hear her sigh, loneliness became a promise to hear her moan, confusion became a resolve to hear her cry out his name.

And he tried, oh, how he tried, to keep himself in check. With ruthless determination, he used every skill he possessed to make her orgasm again and again until he thought she was beyond exhaustion. He stroked, he kissed, he teased, he touched. He ignored her cries asking him to move inside her, hoping against hope that she would soon be too spent to ask him again. Didn't she understand his only concern was her pleasure?

But he hadn't counted on tears. She wasn't the crying type, so when her eyes clenched shut and a single drop slid down her cheek, he was helpless to say no when she asked one more time. Calling himself a coward, he slid into her and found heaven again, if only for this little while.

Eight

Yesterday the park had seemed, if not exactly friendly, at least not malevolent. Today Kerstin felt evil lurking all around her. Every shadow seemed dark and dangerous, every person seemed to be staring at her. Realizing those thoughts were irrational should have helped, but it didn't. She had to force herself to keep walking, keep searching.

Her determination to face her fears was only one of the reasons she'd stubbornly refused to stay with Quinn. The amusing thing was, her decision had nothing to do with what had happened last night. In fact, she was confused by her very lack of self-recrimination. She'd known exactly what she was doing twelve or so hours ago, which was why she'd expected to be a mass of nerves by now.

Instead, although a bit embarrassed by her wanton behavior, she merely needed time alone to sort out her thoughts. She was worried about Quinn, too worried in fact, and it made perfect sense to start distancing herself from him. He had his agenda, and she couldn't let herself get distracted with concern over him. As it was, the urge to talk him out of his vendetta was nearly as strong as her need to find Meghan, and the conflict was pulling her apart.

Her most immediate need was to dispel the persistent image of Quinn as a knight. She'd dreamed of him last night, on a not-quite-white horse, his armor a bit battered. But he'd looked perfect in her mind, and she'd run to him, longing for his arms, only to wake up just before she reached him. She was sure Quinn took her quietness as embarrassment, but her distress was from so much more than that. She had the feeling she'd come so close to touching him, touching his heart, and then he'd been ripped away from her outstretched fingers. She couldn't explain what she was feeling to herself, much less to him, so she'd stayed silent.

She had to give Quinn some knightly credit though, she supposed. He could have used her weakness against her last night, but he hadn't. He'd let her use him, knowing she was seeking a purely physical release from the unendurable pain and the stress. He'd kissed away her demons, just as she'd asked, and guarded her while she slept.

She wished she could hate him for lying to her.

The problem was, she knew the extremes to which she would go to achieve her goal, so she could hardly cast stones at Quinn now. She was most thankful that the truth had come out now, rather than later. Heaven only knew what might have happened to her foolish heart if she hadn't found out in time.

She made another round of the park, this time cutting through the middle to work a small circle in the opposite direction of her last lap.

Around noon, the smell of hamburgers on a vendor's grill lured her closer. The rumbling in her stomach reminded her time was slipping away, and she certainly could not dwell on the fact that she was hopelessly, foolishly in love with Quinn. First things first, she supposed, and that included getting something to eat.

The thought breezed through her mind so casually, she didn't feel the impact until several steps later. Then she stopped in her tracks, frozen in shock. With numb, wooden steps, she searched out a spot to sit down and pulled her knees to her chest convulsively.

No. She shook her head, oblivious to anyone watching her talk to herself. No, no, no, no...

She couldn't be in love with him. That was impossible. He was a complete stranger, even more so now than when she'd met him. He wasn't who or even what she'd thought he was.

For that matter, she wasn't who she thought *she* was anymore.

This couldn't be happening. Of all the times for her

to fall in love, now was not it. She was so close to finding Meghan. So close to putting this nightmare behind her and going back to her safe, comfortable life.

Her fingers curled into a fist, and she gave the ground beside her a good, solid pound. She wasn't going to be in love with him. That was all there was to it. She stood up, ignoring her shaky knees, and repeated to herself firmly, "I am not in love with him. Period. End of discussion."

Throwing her shoulders back, she set off again across the field, her stride determined.

Her knuckles white.

Her skin cold despite the blistering sun.

Kerstin wasn't sure what caught her attention, but her eyes suddenly became riveted on a group of people she was sure she hadn't seen before. Whatever the explanation, her senses became hyperaware, and she turned her head to see if she could better hear the voice she swore was Meghan's.

Following her instincts, she pivoted away from the group and tried to appear casual as she made her way toward the tents housing the arts-and-crafts vendors, stopping as she rounded the last cart in the line. Her hands flew to her mouth to keep from crying out.

It was definitely Meghan.

She was gaunt, her face taut with exhaustion and strain, but Kerstin knew the face that was so similar to her own. Meghan was arguing with a man not quite as tall as Quinn, but from her angle, Kerstin thought he looked just as dangerous. The man wasn't Jackson Pepper—she was sure of that. Pepper was blond, tall and lanky, and this guy was dark, and all broad, powerful muscle.

Picking up a piece of two-by-four from the stack of wood by the vendor cart, probably used to level it, Kerstin snuck closer. Pure, cold determination stole over her, giving her the courage to do whatever had to be done, now that the moment was upon her, to rescue her sister.

She swung the board as hard as she could, connecting with the back of the man's head in a sickening thud. He dropped to the ground with a loud groan.

A second of stunned silence passed before Meghan recognized her.

"Kerstin! What did you do that for?" she cried out, throwing herself to the ground beside the man.

Kerstin stood in stunned silence, unable to believe her eyes. She'd just assaulted a human being to save her sister and instead of grabbing the opportunity for escape, Meghan was crying and brushing the guy's hair out of his face.

"Come on, Travis, wake up."

"Meghan," Kerstin finally managed, rushing forward, "what's the matter with you? Come on, let's get out of here!"

"Not until I know if Travis is all right."

Kerstin threw her hands up in the air. "I can't believe this is happening," she said, kneeling on

Travis's other side. "Meghan, he's breathing, okay? We've got to get out of here."

Meghan didn't move.

"For heaven's sake! This man has kept you prisoner. Who cares if he's hurt?"

Meghan glanced up. "You don't understand. Travis was trying to help me. He's not one of them."

Travis groaned and stirred. He put a hand to his head as he opened his eyes. "What in the—"

He cut himself off as he looked at Meghan, then Kerstin, then back again. He muffled a curse and slowly sat up.

"You must be Kerstin," he said, grunting as he stood.

She nodded. "You'd better go to the hospital," she said warily. "You could have a concussion."

Meghan put her arms around Travis. "She's right. You could be hurt."

"I hurt like hell, but I'll be okay."

Exactly what she'd done to this man struck Kerstin and she put a hand to her roiling stomach.

"I'm so sorry. I can't believe I hit you."

"Kerstin," Travis said gently, but sternly, "pull yourself together. I will be fine, but you're not going to do Meghan or yourself any good if you fall apart."

Kerstin composed herself the best she could and nodded. "You're right. I'll be fine."

Travis smiled encouragingly, and then winced, making Kerstin feel guilty. "You two have got to get out of here. Pepper's probably already looking for us.''

She fought the urge to look over her shoulder. "Where is he?"

"Five or six camps that way," Travis said, nodding his head to the left. "Look, we're out of time! Head for the FBI office in Houston and ask for Matt Newfield. He'll take care of you."

He pushed Meghan away. "Go, Meghan."

"But I don't want—"

"Meghan, just go," he ground out. "I'll find you later."

He thrust her into Kerstin's arms and started walking away. She tightened her hold instinctually as her sister tried to pull away and follow Travis.

"Let me go, Kerstin. He's going to be in danger."

She shook Meghan by the shoulders. "*You're* in danger! We're getting out of here. Now."

Their first few steps were awkward as Meghan kept looking behind her. Kerstin kept a vise grip on Meghan's wrist as they hurried toward Cindy and Jim's camp. Two or three in their large group had driven trucks, and Kerstin was sure someone would lend her a vehicle or give them a ride out of there.

She heard someone call her name and slowed when she saw Quinn hurrying toward her.

He did a double take as he came to a halt and saw Meghan. With aplomb that didn't surprise Kerstin, Quinn held out his hand.

"Hello, I'm Quinn."

He wished he hadn't been so aggressive when Meghan pulled away and inched closer to Kerstin.

"It's all right," she said. "Quinn's been helping me search for you. He's a...friend."

He kept his hand out. Training and experience told him it was a first step for her to even touch his hand, so he kept his grip gentle.

"I'm Meghan. But I guess you knew that."

He smiled, hoping it was a reassuring one. "I wish we were meeting under different circumstances, but I'm still glad to meet you. Listen, I'm sure you've got questions, but we need to get out of here."

Kerstin rolled her eyes. "That's about the tenth time that's been said...and what I'm trying to do!"

Amazed that he could feel humor at a time like this, he flashed Kerstin a touchy-aren't-we grin and took one of each twin's hands in his. He hurried them toward the parking lot. "I've got a truck we can use. We'll grab our things and get you to safety."

They tried to be as inconspicuous as possible as they made their way to a pickup he'd "rented" from a pal of Jim's who had brought a show bike to the rally. Quinn's motorcycle was now in the back—hardly an unusual sight—yet he couldn't rid himself of the feeling they had a neon sign over their heads pointing to them. Hustling the girls inside, he wasted no time getting on the road. An old air conditioner helped to alleviate the heat inside the cab, but nothing could relieve the tension.

He watched the two women as much as he could

while at the same time paying attention to his driving. He was aware the instant Kerstin realized they had actually found Meghan and were getting away. "Oh, Meghan," she said, pulling her twin to her in a fierce hug.

"Kerstin, thank you so much." Tears streamed down her face. "I've been so scared."

"I know, honey," she said as Meghan rested her head on her shoulder. She looked at Quinn. "I'm scared, too. This all seemed too easy."

He nodded. "I know exactly what you mean, but we've got to play the cards as they're dealt. Let's hope we were simply lucky."

Kerstin nodded.

Quinn let Meghan cry for a few moments, knowing it wasn't enough release, but it was all he could afford to let her have until they were out of the woods.

"I hate to start in with the questions so soon, but I need you to tell me as much as you can about what you've seen and heard while you've been with Pepper," Quinn prompted as they sped down the highway.

Meghan wiped her cheeks with the backs of her hands and straightened in the seat.

"Travis said for us to go to the FBI office and not talk to anyone but a friend of his," Meghan said, her voice a little shaky.

Quinn glanced over at Meghan. "Who's Travis?"

She hesitated. "He's been trying to help me."

"He's one of Pepper's men?"

"No...I'm...uh...not sure I'm supposed to talk about it."

"It's okay, Meggie," Kerstin said. "Quinn is a Texas Ranger."

Meghan looked at him. "Are you undercover, too?"

Quinn's eyes darted to her. "Too?"

"Travis is with the Bureau. That's why he told me to go there. He's been trying to get me out of there, but Pepper has been—"

Meghan's body tensed at the very mention of his name.

"It's all right," Quinn assured her. "You're doing fine."

Kerstin didn't share his confidence until her sister took a deep, shuddering breath and seemed to regain her composure. She noticed that Quinn kept glancing in the rearview mirror, and found herself tensing as badly.

"Is someone following us?"

"I can't be sure. The traffic is so heavy, there's no way to know. I'll wind around some side streets before heading to the hotel."

They didn't waste time getting to the room after he pulled into the parking lot.

"Do you think it's safe enough for me to take a shower?" Meghan said, wilting onto the bed as reality caught up with her. Quinn hesitated before compassion overrode his urgency.

"Sure, but make it a quick one."

Kerstin patted her sister's arm before Meghan stood wearily and headed for the bathroom. "I've got an extra set of clothes."

Meghan smiled gratefully and shut the door behind her.

Kerstin paced, as much to avoid looking at Quinn as to soothe her jangled nerves. She forced herself to stop.

"Quinn, I...I really want to thank you. You know Pepper's at the park right now."

He nodded, doing a remarkable job of hiding his thoughts. "You're welcome."

"Are...are you going back?"

He looked away. "I have to."

Without realizing it, she was beside him, her hand on his arm. "Don't, Quinn. Don't go back."

He stepped away, avoiding her outstretched fingers. "I have to. Someone has to see justice served."

"But this is vengeance. Don't you see that? I heard something that now makes sense to me. They said, there is no justice, only mercy."

Quinn rounded on her, his eyes blazing. "Don't you dare say that animal deserves mercy."

"No," she said quietly, putting her hand back on his arm and holding on, "your soul deserves the mercy."

"Then I'm safe, because I have no soul."

She wouldn't let him look away. "You will be the one destroyed by this, Quinn."

Seeing that he had hardened himself to her, she

dropped her hand, but she couldn't stop one last try. "The FBI is obviously closing in on Pepper. Let them punish him."

"I can't take the chance the law will fail again."

"Quinn—"

He pushed past her. "Enough. Just get your sister ready."

He grabbed his bags and went outside.

Kerstin sat in solemn silence as she waited for Meghan. Her elation at saving her sister was tarnished by the knowledge that she couldn't help Quinn. All her bravado aside, she *did* care if he completed his revenge. She cared more than she could have imagined.

She wondered where Quinn had gone, and it took all her willpower not to look out the window and see if he'd left. Her heart knew he would never just abandon her. Not now. Not after all they'd been through.

Still she silently urged Meghan to turn off the water.

As if hearing the silent plea, two loud squeaks of the handles stopped the shower and in moments, the sisters were side by side again, hugging each other desperately.

Meghan didn't ask for time to dry her hair. After combing it, she clasped arms with Kerstin and they headed back to the truck. If Meghan noticed the tension in Quinn's face, she didn't mention it.

Kerstin certainly noticed. And she realized, as he folded a receipt and put it in his wallet, that he'd left the room to settle the bill, not to abscond to parts unknown. But she'd never doubted…

Several frustrating hours later, the three stood beside the borrowed truck once again. It seemed Travis's buddy at the Bureau office was very interested in Meghan's story, but his superior wasn't concerned enough to offer Meghan official protection. Despite Quinn's assurances that nothing motivated Pepper more than revenge, the agent hadn't believed Pepper would take the time to go after Meghan. After taking their statements, the man had urged Meghan and Kerstin to visit relatives who lived out of state and to keep in touch.

Quinn's frustration and anger was almost palpable. He hadn't taken the agent's warning well to stay away from Pepper and his gang.

By the time they had concluded their long session with Special Agent Newfield, evening had taken over. Kerstin was sure, no matter how drained she felt, Meghan had to be past empty.

Worst of all, Kerstin knew she was about to say goodbye to Quinn.

She flinched when he cleared his throat.

"I've been thinking," he began as he moved to lower the tailgate of the pickup. Kerstin didn't realize what he was doing until he pulled a skid out and secured it. "Take this truck and head back to Daddy's. There's a small risk, but I doubt Pepper would connect you to Daddy's Place. I'll tell the owner to pick the truck up there. Anyway, go get your trailer. Head for anywhere but home until you hear from Agent Newfield that everything is…over.''

He didn't look at her as he hopped into the bed, untied the ropes, and carefully eased his bike down from its perch. Once he had the skid back in the bed and the tailgate secured, he pulled a piece of paper out of his pocket and handed it to her with a bank card.

''That's my debit card and the personal ID numbers. Go to the nearest bank and clean it out. You'll have to do it a few hundred dollars a day, as I think there's a limit, but just keep traveling and keep withdrawing until you're safe.''

''Quinn, I can't do—''

''Just shut up and listen.''

She was totally taken aback, unable to utter a retort in her shock.

He scrubbed at his jaw impatiently and gave her a quick glance. ''I'm sorry. I didn't mean to snap. Just please, Kerstin, don't argue with me.''

''I have money of my own, Quinn. I can take care of myself.''

''I'm sure you can, but neither of us knows how this is all going to fall down, so I'm asking you to please take the money. It's the least I owe—''

''You don't owe me anything! Damn it, Quinn—''

''Look, just hear me out. I need to know you'll be far away when I…when this is all over. I don't know how long you'll have to stay away from home so I have to know you'll be provided for. I'm not asking you to understand, I'm just asking you to do it. Please.''

She supposed it didn't matter that she had no intention of taking his money. He needed to think she would, so no one was really hurt in the long run when she said, ''Okay.''

''Promise me.''

Now that was a little bit trickier. She didn't lie. Through all of these days, she'd never fallen that far. ''Um, I promise I'll use this when I need it.''

That seemed to be enough to pacify him because he nodded.

''Head straight for the highway, hear me? Don't go anywhere near the campground.''

It was her turn to nod.

''Okay, then.'' He picked up his helmet and fumbled with it. ''Take care of yourself. I'll get word to you…somehow.''

Her throat was closing up and her eyes were swimming with tears. ''Please, be careful,'' she whispered hoarsely. She wanted to stop him, would have given anything to have that power, but knew she didn't.

Instead of offering false promises, he put his helmet back on his seat and pulled her to him, kissing her fiercely.

''Quinn, I—''

''Kerstin—''

''Don't go.'' She hated herself for saying it, but couldn't stop the words.

He offered no false hope, letting his last, desperate kiss say all that could be said.

Then he set her free and was gone.

Kerstin walked around the truck and settled herself in the driver's seat, holding on to the steering wheel in a death grip as tears streamed down her face. Feeling Meghan's hand on her arm, Kerstin tried to pull herself together.

"Are you all right?"

Snuffling, she wiped her eyes and nodded. "I'm fine."

"Shouldn't we get going?" Meghan asked quietly.

Kerstin responded by starting the engine and heading for the highway.

The words started slowly as the miles began to separate them from the source of their nightmare. Kerstin let Meghan talk the most, listening as she repeated what had been said back at the Bureau office, and adding the details she'd left out of her version to Agent Newfield.

Several times Kerstin had to pull the truck over, her tears undeniable as Meghan relayed a story of a foolish young woman who'd taken a journey into hell. The first few days had been a lark. Then, as quickly as it had begun, it had turned into horror. Pepper seemed to have a Jekyll and Hyde personality. When he was being magnanimous and jovial, he was an incredibly charismatic man. But when he was angry, he became evil incarnate. Meghan had curled up into a ball, sobbing nearly hysterically as she'd recounted again how she'd witnessed Pepper killing a man, completely without remorse, simply because the man had dropped a packet of dope and spilled it.

Kerstin didn't know what to do except hold Meghan close during the more horrid parts of the story. The more she'd talked, the more Kerstin had wanted to turn the truck around and go help Quinn kill Pepper.

Meghan had finally slept, curled up on the tiny space available on the seat, her head on Kerstin's leg. She didn't care if it wasn't exactly a safe thing to do. It was obvious Meghan needed the physical contact, and Kerstin wasn't about to say no.

The problem was, the darkness, the quiet and the thoughts rampaging through her head merely gave her time to worry about Quinn.

Would she ever see him again?

More specifically, would she ever see him alive again?

Nine

Meghan roused from her nap after midnight. "Where are we?" she asked, yawning.

"About an hour from Hell."

The two women looked at each other and hysteria-releasing laughter blurted out of both of them. Before long, they were giggling so hard Kerstin had to pull into a truck stop until the spasms finally eased. By mutual consent, they went inside for a break and a cup of coffee.

The small restaurant boasted cracked vinyl booths, but the floors and tabletops were shiny and clean, something that surprised Kerstin. She didn't complain, though, as she accepted a cup of coffee from a sleepy waitress and simply sat for a moment, looking at the sister she had been afraid she'd lost.

Meghan grabbed her hand and Kerstin squeezed back, needing the tactile proof that this wasn't a dream just as much as her twin did.

"I was so afraid," she finally managed to say.

Meghan nodded. "I can't believe it's over."

"Well, it's not over yet, but at least we're out of there." She doctored her coffee to give her time to compose herself, and finally cleared her throat. "Meggie, do you want to talk some more?"

A minute passed before Meghan looked up from stirring her cup. "I'm not really feeling anything, you know?" Her brow furrowed in confusion. "I can't seem to think straight."

"You're still in shock, honey. It's going to be a while—"

"Oh, I know. It's just…oh, never mind. You'll think I'm crazy."

"No, I won't. I promise."

"Well, it's just that…what I'm really worried about is Travis. He's in so much danger."

Kerstin listened as Meghan described how Travis had come into the picture just after she and Pepper had gotten together. She'd had no idea he was an agent until Pepper had turned psycho on her. It was painful to hear Meghan describe the misery she'd suffered at Pepper's hands, but Kerstin was acting on instinct. She was no psychologist, but she thought it was probably better to get Meghan talking about it right away. If Meghan started burying things, who knew how much worse the scars would be?

The urge to hurt the man who'd harmed her sister came over her again, as Kerstin listened to more of Meghan's story. There were moments when Kerstin truly understood Quinn's motives for revenge.

"You just don't understand how compelling he can be," Meghan was saying, sounding almost desperate.

"Travis?" Kerstin asked, confused.

"No, Jackson."

Even that made her stumble mentally. She'd never called Pepper anything but his surname in her mind.

"You're right, Meggie, I can't understand since I haven't been near the guy, but I promise I believe you."

"He's a control freak. He got a big kick out of tormenting me. I didn't know how long I was going to be a novelty, though, and was always wondering if today was going to be the day he'd get tired and—"

"Don't say it, Meggie."

She sniffled and wiped her nose with her napkin. "I told him I could get him money if he didn't hurt me." She twisted the napkin in her fingers. "I kept trying to think of ways to buy time."

"Meggie, I would have given him everything I have," Kerstin said, tugging on Meghan's hand so she'd look up. "You know that, don't you?"

Meghan nodded. "I kept thinking if he'd stop long enough to send you a ransom note I'd be able to get away. He never did."

The conversation lulled for a long moment. Kerstin

wasn't sure what to say so she let Meghan decide the next direction to take.

Meghan finally continued. "Travis thought I was part of the gang at first, and he wasn't very nice at all. As soon as he figured out that Jackson wasn't letting me go, he made it look as though he didn't like me even more, but he really did. Like me, I mean. Jackson made him my guard, thank God."

Kerstin tried to sort through it all. "You're saying that Travis maneuvered his way into being your guard by acting as though he didn't like you?"

Meghan nodded. "He even slapped me one time." Fury welled in Kerstin, but Meghan hurried to reassure her. "Listen, Kerstin, if he hadn't made Jackson truly believe his act, you have no idea what those guys might have done to me. Jackson probably would have already killed me by now. Travis has apologized so many times, I can't tell you, but in the situation, he really had no choice. I've had a lot of time to think about it, and I think Travis is the only reason I'm not stark raving insane."

Kerstin tried to understand, and hoped Meghan's sympathies and loyalties weren't misguided. Just because Travis was an FBI agent didn't make him a saint, and she was worried about Meghan's obvious attachment to the man.

"I'm sure he was doing what he thought he had to," she said placatingly.

She changed the subject by describing Daddy and what to expect when they arrived in Hell. Meghan listened attentively, but didn't hesitate to change the subject at a timely pause.

"So, what aren't you telling me about this Quinn guy?"

Kerstin's one semester of drama in high school failed abysmally as she tried to look innocent. "What's to tell? I already said he's a Texas Ranger, or was one, anyway. He's after Pepper for killing his wife, and he helped me find you. End of story."

"Then why won't you look at me when you talk about him?"

"No reason."

"Except that you're in love with him."

Kerstin blustered, "What are you talking about? I hardly know the guy!"

"Well, I hardly know Travis, but I know I love him."

"We'll talk about that later, when you've had time to recover—"

"Don't try to tell me that I don't love him. Travis tried to tell me that, too, but I know what I feel."

"Meggie—"

"I saw how you looked at Quinn, and I saw his face after he kissed you. He loves you, too."

"That's insane. He doesn't feel anything but relief that he can get on with his mission."

"Kerstin—"

"I don't want to talk about this. We need to get back on the road anyway, so finish your coffee and let's go. Time is still not our friend."

Both women spent the last hour of their trip lost in thought. Kerstin's worry about her sister's emotional attachments only made her own feelings for Quinn seem equally uncertain. Had she merely done her own version of the misguided, misplaced affection she was afraid Meghan had? What made her feelings any more sane than Meghan's?

They pulled into Daddy's back driveway, bone-tired and emotionally wiped out. To his credit, Daddy took Kerstin's reappearance with little surprise. He knew as well as she did that as little time should be spent in one place as possible, but it was also obvious that the two women couldn't go on driving without some sleep. A phone call from Daddy had several of his "boys" there in no time, and Kerstin and Meghan lay down on the bed in her trailer to sleep in relative safety.

Daylight came all too soon. After calling her father and letting him know everything was all right, Kerstin dressed in clean clothes, slipping Quinn's bank card into her shirt pocket. She was determined to turn it in at the first branch office she came to.

In a style uniquely his, Daddy finally explained why he'd gotten involved. He pulled a picture from his wallet and Kerstin and Meghan looked in amazement at a photo of a young woman who resembled them in features and hair color. She wasn't a carbon copy, by any means, but they could see how Daddy had taken Kerstin as a close match to his daughter. It seemed that Daddy hadn't seen his child in some years, and nostalgia and coincidence were the sole reasons he'd been so willing to step in when Kerstin first appeared.

After giving her massive benefactor a big hug, and offering him her hope that he saw his little girl again, Kerstin took the wheel of her own truck once more. Meghan settled into the passenger side, the trailer following dutifully behind. Daddy would take care of contacting the man who owned the borrowed wheels.

For no other reason than they'd never been to the mountains, Kerstin and Meghan agreed to head for Colorado. It was as good a place as any to rest and recuperate while they waited to get the all-clear from the FBI.

They hadn't been on the road long when Kerstin noticed a group of bikers coming up behind them in her side mirrors. She smiled.

"Those guys," she said with mock censure.

"What guys?" Meghan said, taking her eyes from her magazine to glance in her own mirror.

"Daddy probably sent them to drive with us for a while up the highway. He's worse than our own father about being protective."

Meghan had marveled at the story, just as Kerstin had, but they both had been duly appreciative of the good fortune whether it made sense or not.

Traveling in the right lane since her trailer forced her to keep a more cautious speed, Kerstin didn't start to get scared until the bikers pulled on both sides of her. Her hackles itched to see two people riding on the shoulder. She didn't recognize them, although that wasn't surprising, but suddenly things didn't feel right.

Her immediate thought was a wish for Quinn. She hated herself for her cowardice, but she'd have given anything for his strong, comforting presence at the moment.

Kerstin's tension became apparent, and as the bikers forced the truck off the road, Meghan began to scream.

Quinn had no idea how fast he was going. He'd replaced his speedometer back in the days when the law didn't allow them to go higher than 80 mph, so it was no help. The only thing that kept him from running his bike wide-open was that he would do Kerstin no good dead. Or Meghan, of course.

He couldn't recall ever feeling a rage so cold that he was calm. Not even the fury that had fueled him since Haley's death had been this complete. He was amazed that he could review how smoothly Pepper had played him for a chump and still not feel anything.

The memory of going back to the campground last night should have frustrated him all over again. With it being the night of the big concert, the grounds had been a mass of milling people no longer clumped in haphazard groups. Pepper's minions hadn't found him—talk about irony—until the crowds had started thinning sometime after three o'clock. They'd delivered a note saying, "Go to Hell, Ranger O'Byrne."

He was sure Pepper thought he was a comedic genius, but Quinn knew with a cold, hard pain in his gut this was no toss-off curse.

Knowing Kerstin and Meghan were probably already at Daddy's by the time he'd gotten the note, Quinn had had no choice but to head for Hell. He'd had no sleep in over twenty-four hours, but he hit the road, not stopping longer than it took to make a pit stop, fill his tank and grab something to drink. Now the Monday morning sunshine nearly blinded him, but that wasn't the only reason he was squinting behind his sunglasses.

At the edge of Hell, he'd been flagged down. The man had told him which direction Pepper and his men had gone, and had relayed the message, "Come and get me." Quinn resisted the urge to punch the messenger's lights out and hadn't stopped since.

The little town Pepper had headed to was deserted. In its heyday, oil had been king in Sunflower, and the town boasted a good number of warehouses which were now long abandoned and in questionable condition.

And Kerstin could be in any one of them.

Quinn found a high vantage point above the town and squatted on his haunches. Through binoculars he'd borrowed from Daddy, he saw a congregation of motorcycles in front of a two-story building of rusted prefab. That didn't mean anyone was actually in that location, of course, but it did give him a rough idea that he had around ten "problems" to contend with.

"I've been waiting for you."

Quinn whirled, nearly having a stroke before he recognized Sonny.

"Bickler, I oughta take your head off for that."

Sonny shivered in mock fear. "And you could be dead for being stupid," he countered. "You didn't even know I was here. What if I'd been Pepper or one of his goons?"

"Well, you're not, so drop it. What are you doing here, anyway? And how did you get here ahead of me?"

Sonny dropped down with Quinn to a less obvious position. "I'm hoping to help you and stop you from screwing up a year's worth of undercover work."

Quinn kept his mouth shut.

"You see, my friend, the Bureau has been after Pepper longer than you have." Sonny gave him an arch look. "Yes, I know you're out for revenge, but I haven't exactly had a chance to chat with you about it. When I saw you the other night with Weaver, I called Austin and spoke with your partner."

"And Randy told you what?"

Sonny studied the terrain a little too intently. "Helluva guy, your partner. Took me convincing him your sorry hide was in a lot of hot water before he'd give me more than a hint of why you were down here."

Quinn loosed a frustrated breath. "This is all fascinating, but get to the point."

"The point is, the Bureau knew Pepper had the Lundquist woman. We have a man in his operation who's been keeping an eye on her—"

"I know. A guy named Travis."

"Right. He was waiting for an opportunity to get her away without blowing the operation and/or getting them both killed. He was, in fact, trying to get Meghan away when her sister showed up and plowed him across the back of the head with a two-by-four. Of all the nightmares, Meghan wasn't going to leave because she decided she was in love with him, and he was in danger. It nearly blew the whole operation right then and there."

"Nearly?"

"Travis went back with a very convincing lump on the back of his head, and Pepper sent people out looking for the women. Somebody saw you and the girls walking across the park, and reported back to Pepper."

"How do you know so much?"

"Travis was able to get word to me as they headed out to follow the girls. They made the mistake of stopping for a long time at a truck stop and it gave Pepper time to catch up. The girls made it into Hell and had some protection that night, but when they took off this morning, they were wide-open. I haven't been far behind all morning."

Sonny shifted to look Quinn in the eyes. "The long and short of it is, we're about to drop the net on the biggest sting in history in this part of the country, and you may have just single-handedly managed to screw it up. Somebody's going to have your butt in a sling if this comes down hard.''

Quinn nodded, accepting responsibility for his actions without question. ''But what I'm worried about right now is the innocent people in that building.''

A scream shattered the quiet, and Quinn jerked forward reactively. Only Sonny's strong hand on his arm kept him from charging down the hillside.

''Don't be an idiot! You're outnumbered at least six to one. Wait until my SWAT team arrives.''

''Look, Sonny, you can wait if you want to. If I'm lucky, I'll lessen the odds for your men when they get here.''

Quinn hurried to his faring and retrieved the gun and clip he'd gotten from Daddy, as well as checking his own weapon. He kept his gun in his hand and slipped the other into his belt.

He heard the distinct sound of a round being chambered and turned to find himself staring down the barrel of Sonny's SIG-Sauer.

He didn't even flinch. ''I hope you're ready to kill me, because I'm going down there.''

''Don't make me do it, man,'' Sonny said. ''I can't let you jeopardize this because of your vendetta.''

Quinn actually laughed. ''Right now, the only thing I care about is the woman I love. Every second we argue is one more second Pepper is going to get tired of waiting for me.''

Sonny's brow furrowed in confusion. The gun lowered. "Waiting for you?"

"I thought you knew what was going on."

"I do. At least, I thought I did. When Pepper stopped here, we figured Travis's cover had gotten blown and put Pepper onto the sting. We figured he's using the girls as hostages for leverage, although we haven't received any demands yet."

"Well, you're wrong. I'd bet, unless you're right about Travis's cover being blown, that Pepper has no idea the Bureau's breathing down his neck. The psycho left me messages to come and get him, taunting me with holding Kerstin and Meghan."

Sonny nodded thoughtfully. "The lookout who saw you walking with the girls must have recognized you."

"And he made sure I got the message to follow him, and by damn, here I am."

Sonny was thinking. "Although my first concern is, of course, the hostages, this could actually work out without blowing the whole operation." He gave Quinn a hard look. "You've got to wait for the team, man. We'll get the girls out."

Quinn scowled. "As soon as Pepper hears a helicopter or sees the attack coming, he'll start killing and run."

"My guys are the best—"

"I'm sure they are, Sonny, but I'm not betting Kerstin's life on it. Or Meghan's."

He started walking, fairly certain Sonny was going

to let him go. He was tense, knowing if Sonny was going to shoot, he'd do it any second now. It was evident a moment later, as he made his way down the hill using the cover of trees and shrubs, that the agent wasn't going to interfere.

Kerstin wondered why she wasn't more afraid. By all rights, she should be quivering in terror. She was tied back-to-back with her sister around a wooden support pole in the middle of a smelly abandoned warehouse. Her jaw ached and her left eye was swelling. Rope had been wound around them at chest level like something out of a bad movie, but she supposed there was some comfort that her hands weren't tied. A madman sat on a pile of wood that had been left against the wall, seeming for all the world as if he hadn't a care. Meghan was crying softly, trying to get a beaten and bloody Travis at her feet to wake up.

So, why wasn't she in hysterical tears? Nothing in her thirty-four years had prepared her for this. She hadn't taken any ''How To Be A Hostage'' classes in college so she guessed she would have to play this one by ear.

She kept her expression blank but struggled to hide a snort of laughter. She must truly have gone nuts if the urge to laugh was hitting her at a moment like this. But what else was she supposed to do? If she thought about Quinn walking into this much-too-obvious trap, she really would go insane.

She glanced at her captor, wishing she could do

something besides stand there helplessly, even though just looking at him made cold fear settle in her stomach. She'd forgotten how smooth Pepper was. Even in the "uniform" of black jeans and T-shirt, he stood out among his entourage. His blond hair was expensively styled, his skin well tended, his boots polished. Maybe it was that he appeared so normal that made this all the more frightening. The illusion remained that she could talk to him logically, convince him how foolish this whole idea was, but the pain in her cheek testified to the fallacy in that line of thought.

Her attempts at logic had earned his laughter, and her attempts to bribe him with the stocks and cash she had available had garnered her the back of his hand across her face. She'd never been struck in her life and the pain had ripped through her, shocking her into silence. His unperturbed expression as he'd hit her had scared her more than anything. The man was simply evil, and she had no doubt he would kill Quinn with equally little reaction.

As if her thought had conjured him, a noise came from the next room. The unmistakable sound of fighting filtered through, first a crash, then a thud. It seemed forever before Quinn was shoved into the room toward Pepper's "throne." Then she wanted to cry. It was small comfort that the two men hauling Quinn were in obvious pain when a bruise was already blackening Quinn's eye, his shirt was torn, and his shoulder was bloody where he'd obviously been thrown to the rough concrete.

He met her eyes and a twitch of his lip was probably meant to reassure her, but it failed. He glanced at Meghan, but looked quickly away without reaction.

Pepper spoke to one of the men before facing Quinn. "You took down three of my guys? Not bad, Ranger. Unfortunately not good enough."

While Pepper spoke, Kerstin watched a change come over Quinn. He exuded total confidence, his stance almost casual, as if he and Pepper were having a simple conversation, as if three people besides Pepper weren't pointing loaded guns at him.

"Come closer," Pepper invited with a sweep of his arm. "Let's chat, shall we?"

Quinn moved farther into the room, but remained silent.

"You know, Ranger," he said, releasing the magazine from his pistol and snapping it back in an intimidating manner, "you have caused me a lot of trouble."

"That breaks my heart," Quinn said.

Kerstin held her breath at his wisecrack, her heart lurching in worry. Didn't he know he was being sarcastic to a madman?

"I'm glad to hear that," Pepper quipped back, placing his gun next to his thigh and accepting a knife from one of his henchmen.

"Not a bad-looking blade," he said casually, using the tip to clean under his fingernails. "Not exactly Ranger issue, though."

"But good enough to cut your heart out."

Kerstin tried to tell Quinn with her eyes to be careful, but Quinn kept his attention focused on their captor.

"I didn't know I was going to get a second shot at you, Ranger," he commented softly, changing subjects without warning. Then he straightened and laughed. "I wish you could see your face. You look worse than that day in court." Pepper's phony smile faded. The ensuing snarl was even more chilling. "You remember that day, don't you, Ranger?"

He advanced with the knife.

"Like it was yesterday," Quinn taunted, despite the sharp blade tip pressing into the soft skin under his chin.

She had to make herself breathe as she watched small drops of blood slide down Quinn's neck. Her fear was reaching the point of frustrated panic. Pepper apparently hadn't gotten the reaction from Quinn he'd been looking for. He stepped away from Quinn and circled her, forcing Kerstin to twist her head around to see what he was doing. He stopped by Meghan and used his fingers to lift her chin.

Kerstin nearly screamed when he moved his face close to Meghan's, and said with menacing softness, "Quit sniveling." Meghan tried to obey, but was obviously beyond the point of coherent thought. He raised his hand back to slap her.

"Pepper! Why don't you just save that energy for me, huh? We've got a lot to discuss."

Pepper changed his blow to a too-forceful pat on the cheek to let Quinn know he hadn't been fooled, but at least for now, he was distracted. Kerstin added one more thing to a growing list to thank Quinn for when they got out of there.

If they got out of there...

Pepper moved as fast as the snake she knew he was. With his own laugh, he turned and threw Quinn's knife in one smooth motion. She barely contained a squeak of fear as the blade imbedded in the wood mere inches from her head and now quivered to a stop. Dusting his hands, Pepper moved back to his seat, not stopping Quinn when he moved a few steps closer.

Kerstin took his brief glance and held it to her heart. She was trying to be brave, but Quinn's dance with this cobra was making her tremble. She noted that the three men who answered to Pepper were keeping as silent and still as she, although they kept their weapons trained on Quinn.

"While I was waiting for you to arrive," Pepper said, shifting into a more comfortable position, "I was wondering how I wanted this to all fall into place. I see myself as a director, you see, and this is our stage."

Quinn seemed to lose patience. "Come on, Pepper,

isn't it about time for you to tell me how you're going to kill me and make me pay, blah, blah, blah…''

Pepper raised an eyebrow. ''I'm supposed to believe you don't care about your friends here?'' He pointed in Kerstin's direction. He continued before Quinn could answer. ''You want to know what's really hilarious? I didn't even connect you to the twins here until my man saw you with them in the park. By the way it's not very smart to give someone your bank card.''

He enjoyed the confusion in Quinn's eyes. ''Then I found your card—had to search her for weapons, you understand.''

Quinn didn't react to Pepper's taunt, but Kerstin couldn't help shivering in memory of his hands on her body, and her terror when he'd found the card.

Pepper shrugged and continued. ''Needless to say, I had to include you in my plans to get that traitorous little bitch back.'' Pepper's eyes were hard as he stared at Meghan. ''No one messes with my plans, and you three have caused me a lot of aggravation.

''So,'' he concluded loudly, his smile transforming his face into a parody of joy, ''all that remains is to kill your little friends, enjoy watching you watch them die, then dispatching you to your final reward. I won't make it easy, however, as I want to see your face as I walk away a free man. Again.''

Quinn's laughter was as bright, and frightening, as Pepper's expression. "You are such a lunatic."

"Please," Pepper said with feigned indignation, "the term is *psychopath*. But enough small talk. Is there anything you'd like to know about my little date with your wife before I take another woman away from you?"

Kerstin bit her lip as Quinn jerked forward a bit, but caught himself.

How he kept from flying across the room at Pepper's head, Kerstin would never know.

The sound of breaking glass high above them answered her confusion. The sound of a gunshot reverberated through the room and the man next to Pepper cried out as he fell. The rest was a blur.

Pepper dove for cover, taking his gun. Quinn dove, too, rolling near her. She ducked as a bullet struck the wood over her head, even as she struggled frantically against the ropes.

A man ran past them, tossing a gun toward Quinn. Under a deafening round of shots, Quinn leaped up, wrenching the knife from the pole.

"Head for cover," he shouted to her, jerking his head toward a pile of lumber as he hacked through the ropes.

Kerstin's numb legs collapsed under her, and Meghan collapsed on top of Travis. Crawling to her sister, Kerstin shielded them as best she could.

The henchmen quickly gave up to the federal

agents who swarmed into the room, but Pepper was nowhere to be seen.

"Quinn, over here," she screamed as Pepper's head appeared over a different pile of boards.

Kerstin grabbed a fallen pipe and threw it in Pepper's direction. It flew wide, and in the next heartbeat, Pepper lunged toward her over the lumber. She screamed again as he grabbed her and dragged her to her feet.

Quinn stopped cold. He'd been racing for her, but Pepper had been closer.

Pepper's arm was around her neck so tightly she choked, and everyone in the room seemed to freeze.

"Well, now," Pepper said, breathing raggedly, pressing the muzzle of his gun into her already sore throat. She strained away from the hot tip burning her neck.

Quinn never took his eyes off of Pepper. His aim at Pepper's forehead never wavered.

"Drop it, Ranger."

"More bad dialogue, Pepper?"

"I'll kill her."

"You'll be dead, too."

Deathly silence surrounded them as their eyes stayed locked, and thoughts whirled through Quinn's head. The one that surprised him was the decision to kill Pepper only if he hurt Kerstin. With a calm that seemed out of place, he knew in that split second that this was no longer about revenge, but about saving lives. His need to kill had been replaced by a will to live. The thirst to punish Pepper still sang in his veins, but the need to kill was gone, replaced by a renewal of an oath he'd taken a long time ago. He would save Kerstin not only because he loved her, but because that was his job. And he wouldn't take a life if he didn't have to for the very same reasons.

He only hoped he'd have the opportunity to tell Kerstin how profoundly she'd changed his life.

Kerstin twisted against Pepper's grip and bit his arm. Pepper yelled in pain and let go reflexively. She dropped to the ground.

Pepper roared with anger and shifted his gun to follow her down.

And Quinn squeezed his trigger.

Pepper exploded backward, red already staining the cloth over his right shoulder. Quinn ran to kick Pepper's gun out of reach. His arm was useless, but Quinn wouldn't take any chances.

The room erupted in movement. Black-clothed SWAT members took the henchmen away and took custody of Pepper. Sirens sounded and the *whop-whop* of a helicopter came closer.

But all Quinn could see was Kerstin. He hardly recognized Sonny speaking to him, and surrendered his gun as if in a daze. He didn't stop walking until he reached her. She was curled over her legs, sobbing. He knelt beside her and took her into his arms.

"Shh, it's over now. You're all right."

Surging against him, she cried even harder. Quinn stroked her head, alone in a sea of people.

"Oh, Quinn, I thought—"

"Shh. I'm all right. Are you okay? Are you hurt?"

She shook her head. "I'm not hurt. Is Pepper…"

"He's bleeding, but he's alive."

She put her hands against his face, as if trying to convince herself he was real. "I can't…I thought—"

He tried to soothe her again. "I'm fine, Kerstin."

It took several minutes of embracing her tightly for her to calm down enough to believe him. He understood, as he needed time himself to simply hold her and absorb the knowledge that his words were no mere platitude.

Kerstin finally lifted her head from his shoulder.

"I'm glad he's not dead."

Surprised, Quinn pulled his head back so he could see her face. "Why?"

"Because I didn't want you to have anything more on your conscience." Kerstin looked over to where Meghan and Travis were being placed on gurneys. Her gaze hardened as she looked at Pepper. "And because he doesn't deserve the easy way out."

"Don't hold your anger for too long, sweetheart. It will make you bitter, and he doesn't deserve that much of your soul." Quinn pulled her close. "Trust me. I know."

She nodded, but stayed silent.

Quinn saw his partner and Sonny beckoning him over. Reluctantly he stood and helped her to her feet.

"I've got to go. Some men are going to talk to you and will get you and Meghan home."

"You won't—" She cut herself off. "Of course not. You'll be too busy." She threw her arms around his neck. "Thank you, Quinn. For everything."

His arms tightened around her. "No, thank you. You gave me back my soul, and I'll always be grateful."

Relinquishing Kerstin to the agent who had come forward to escort her out, Quinn watched his heart leave as she walked away.

Ten

Kerstin stared at her computer screen, not seeing the half-drafted report. Instead, she kept hearing Quinn's last words to her repeating over and over in her mind: *You gave me back my soul, and I'll always be grateful.*

He'd also told her she'd be all right....

Physically, he'd been proven correct. The blisters on her neck had healed, the bruises had disappeared, but the ache in her heart seemed to get worse every day. If he was so grateful, why hadn't he called?

She wanted to tell him he'd given her something incredible, too. He'd shown her not only to let go of the past, but even more astounding, he'd awakened a passionate place in her she hadn't even known existed. Time had helped her sort through the myriad events, and Kerstin had realized how rigid her thinking had been, how static her life-style.

She'd learned so much about herself, had reevaluated what she wanted out of life. She wanted so much to call Quinn and share her revelations with him, but she was too afraid.

She glanced at Meghan, sitting on the sofa Kerstin kept in her home office, idly flipping through a magazine. Meghan had made great changes, too. She wouldn't have planned going through the ordeal she'd endured, but good things were happening now that it was over.

When the doorbell rang, Meghan jumped nearly a foot, and Kerstin hurried over to put a reassuring hand on her sister's shoulder.

"Calm down. Everything's going to be fine."

Twisting her fingers in her lap, Meghan's face was a mask of misery. "What if he doesn't feel anything for me anymore? What if he thinks I'm ugly? I've lost so much weight."

It was true that the ensuing weeks had taken a toll on Meghan's health. Not a large woman to begin with, she'd gotten dangerously thin during her recuperation and therapy. She was slowly replacing the much-needed pounds, but her face was still gaunt and her bones too sharp.

"You look beautiful," Kerstin assured her sister.

And, truth be told, Meghan did look beautiful. Her face was flushed with excitement, her hair was soft and glossy. It had grown out a bit and she'd brushed it back from her face, leaving a wispy bang over her forehead. It made her look young, and framed her eyes perfectly. The flowing rayon dress she'd chosen flared from an empire waist and did a lot to camouflage her thinness.

Kerstin knelt in front of her sister and took her hands. "Listen to me. The only reason Travis hasn't been here sooner is because he told you he was going to give you time to heal. Give him a chance."

The bell chimed again and Kerstin stood. "I'll go get that. You take some deep breaths and come out in a minute."

She hurried to the front of the house and opened the door to smile at the man who'd saved Meghan's life.

"Hello, Travis." She only hesitated a second before hugging him warmly. "Please, come in."

"You look wonderful," the tall man said. He'd lost his own fair share of weight.

"Thank you, so do you," she said, then motioned toward the cane he carried. "Is that going to be permanent?"

"The doctor doesn't think so. The bullet really reamed some muscle tissue in my thigh, but it should heal in time."

"I'm glad." She studied her nails for a moment. "You know, Travis, I'll never be able to thank you—"

"Don't, Kerstin. You've thanked me enough by

keeping me informed on Meghan's progress over these past couple of months. I think I'd have gone crazy if—"

"Now it's my turn to say stop. I haven't told Meghan how often we've spoken. She had so much to get through, and has a lot of therapy she needs to complete, so I only told her you checked on her occasionally. I shouldn't ask this, but—"

"I'll be gentle with her, I promise."

Kerstin nodded. She couldn't shield Meghan forever. The therapist had said being overprotective would be the most damaging thing she could do, so Kerstin had done her best to make Meghan feel safe but not smothered. The rest of the healing was up to Meghan and the therapist, so Kerstin had tried to stay out of the way. It had been a blessing beyond measure to see Meghan respond quickly to the weekly sessions.

"Have you talked to Quinn?" Travis asked after Kerstin led him to the living room and invited him to sit.

She shook her head, unable to speak around the knot that had formed in her throat. If Travis had asked if she'd thought about Quinn, however, the answer would have been every minute of every day. Or at least it seemed like it. His face was indelibly etched in her mind. The sound of his voice played in her dreams. The memory of his touch made her shiver in a warm room.

"Have you?" she asked, maybe a bit too casually.

"Sure. We had to wrap up the investigation so we talked quite a bit. I'm just grateful he came away from this with a simple reprimand. He's a good man."

Due to his efforts to save them all that day, Travis had told her, Quinn had proven he was no killer. Other than some flack for disobeying orders, the Department of Public Safety was still blessed with a fine Ranger. Travis had hinted that Quinn might retire, but Kerstin couldn't think about that. It was all she could do not to cry herself to sleep every night without worrying about Quinn throwing away his career.

She'd hoped time would prove her feelings for him were an infatuation, but every day showed her soul had been given completely to a man who had no interest in her. Other than calling to check on Meghan once or twice, she hadn't heard from him, and she was doing everything in her power to convince her wayward heart she needed to move on.

A sound at the door captured their attention. Travis stood when he saw Meghan, and Kerstin only had to take one look at how they stared at each other to know everything was going to be all right. Meghan practically flew across the carpet and into Travis's arms. As they kissed, Kerstin left and picked her keys and purse up off the counter in the kitchen. They didn't need a chaperon, and even if she were in another room, she was afraid they'd feel crowded.

A drive suddenly seemed like a good idea. It was a gloriously crisp November afternoon. Not a cloud marred the pristine blue sky, and the air was cool enough for a coat. She thought about going shopping, but that didn't really appeal to her restless mood. She could go into work, but she was going to continue on half days through the end of the year and didn't want to send her boss mixed signals. It was the best thing for her own recovery, and it also meant Meghan wasn't alone all day. Kerstin was realizing how long it took to get over an ordeal of this nature, and was grateful she had the opportunity to take it slowly, for her sake as well as Meghan's.

Kerstin found herself on I-35, north of the 183 interchange, before she even realized where she was going. She drove this stretch of highway every morning to go to her office, but she couldn't seem to keep her eyes from searching out the unprepossessing red-brick building housing the DPS. Maybe she thought she'd catch a glimpse of him getting in or out of his car, or maybe spot him on the road, but it never happened.

Maybe she should call. It had been over two months...

But every time she picked up the phone, she got a case of the nerves that made Meghan's seem like playacting.

As she neared the brick building, she put on her signal and turned into the front parking lot. She'd never been so indecisive in her life, and it was beginning to bother her. Maybe the answer wasn't a phone call at all. Maybe it was taking the bull by the horns, or some other appropriate cliché, and just acting on the impulse.

With a fortifying breath, she stepped out of her car and went inside. She stopped at the reception desk.

"Hello—" she glanced at the nameplate "—Betty. Is Sergeant O'Byrne available?"

The woman gave her a professionally courteous smile. "Is he expecting you?"

"No, he's not."

"I can see if he's in his office. And your name?"

The moment of truth. Did she back out now, while she had the chance?

The backbone she'd been missing these past few months reasserted itself. "Please tell him Kerstin Lundquist is here."

Betty's eyes widened. Then her smile turned decidedly warmer. "I tell you what…let's surprise him."

She led Kerstin down several corridors and around several corners. She pointed to a door, patting Kerstin's arm before pivoting and heading back the way she'd come.

Kerstin had little choice now. She wondered if she could even find her way out. With her luck, she'd end up in some secret room and get arrested, so she found the courage, somewhere, to move and stand in the open doorway.

He was at his desk, his head bent as he wrote on the pages in front of him. The crisply ironed Western shirt was a far cry from the T-shirts she'd known him to wear, but it suited him. The moss green did wonders for his coloring.

She didn't know why, but his office surprised her. It was larger than she'd been expecting, for one thing. An off-white couch and chair formed a seating area in the front of his desk, and there was still plenty of room behind his chair for a credenza. Awards and framed diplomas graced the walls, and a bookcase held what appeared to be a collection of law and history books.

But she didn't look at anything for long except the man. She drank in the sight of him, filling her parched heart with his dark hair, now cut severely short, with his broad shoulders, with his strong, graceful hands. Chickening out, she stepped back to walk away, but the movement caught his attention.

He looked up and she froze in place as his eyes locked with hers.

He stood slowly, never taking his eyes away. She'd forgotten they were so blue.

Finally he spoke. "Kerstin."

That was it. One word. Her name. But said in a soft whisper, almost like a prayer.

"Quinn."

"Come in."

Mobilized, he moved around his desk to usher her inside and close his door. He took the chair next to the couch, letting her choose how close she sat.

She chose the cushion nearest him.

"How are you?"

She smiled. Okay, they could do the small talk thing if they needed to. "Fine. Meghan's fine. Travis is fine. In fact, the reason I'm out bumming around is they're lip-locked in my living room right now. I felt like a voyeur."

"I'm glad you came by."

She couldn't do it. She couldn't play games anymore. She had to know. If she was supposed to go home, lick her wounds and get on with life without him, then fine. But she had to know now.

"Are you? Glad I'm here, I mean?"

His brow furrowed. "Of course I am."

"Then why haven't you called me?"

He looked away. "I did—"

"To check on Meghan, not to talk to me."

He fidgeted and Kerstin could tell he wanted to get up and pace. She was pleased when he didn't.

"I...I didn't know if you'd want me to. After everything—"

"After you saved my life? And my sister's?"

"It's not that simple..."

"Isn't it? Or are you trying to tell me it would be better if I left?"

"Better?" He closed his eyes and gave a hoarse laugh. "Kerstin, do you know how many nights I've dreamed of seeing you again? Of being this near to you, smelling your perfume, wanting to touch you so badly I'm about to explode?"

"No, I don't know. Tell me."

"Every night. Every single night. My nightmares

have been replaced with dreams of holding you. Now it's the days I dread because I have to face the hours alone.''

"Well, I'm here now.''

He opened his eyes. "I know.''

"Then why won't you hold me?''

"Because I don't know where to go from here. If you walk out of my life again, I'll…I'll—''

"Die?''

He nodded.

"Then you know how I feel. Do you need me to say it first, Quinn?''

He tensed, as if waiting for a blow.

She took one last, fortifying breath. "All right, then. I love you.''

Looking stunned, he just sat there as if that wasn't at all what he was expecting her to say. "What?''

"Have you gone deaf? I said I love you.''

In the next instant, she found herself plastered backward on the sofa in a crushing embrace. She met his kiss with all the fervor more than two months of uncertainty and prayer had built inside of her. She was breathless by the time he lifted his head, his smile radiant as he looked down at her.

"Say it again.''

She tried to appear indignant, but it was hard in her present position. "Not until you say it.''

He kissed her senseless again instead, his fingers making a mess of her hair.

She pushed against his shoulder until he finally relented and backed off. "Say it."

He swept her hair behind her ear and ran a callused thumb down her jaw. "I love you."

Another minute of furiously mating lips and tongues was his reward. He finally let her sit up, and she tried to hide her disappointment. It probably was a smart thing, though. In another few seconds they would no doubt have spontaneously combusted.

Quinn compromised by pulling her onto his lap.

She wrapped her arms around his neck, a precious flicker of hope leaping in her heart. She knew they had sexual chemistry between them, but was that enough to build a relationship on? If the ordeal had taught her anything at all, it was that life was precious, and she wasn't going to waste one more second with unanswered questions.

"Quinn?"

"Hmm?" he said, distracted from his exploration of the top buttons of her blouse.

"Now that we've got the big question out of the way, there's a few others we need to discuss."

"You mean like how soon we can get married?"

"Married? You haven't even asked me yet."

"Well, will you?"

"I don't know. Now be serious," she scolded, taking his hands away from the front hook of her bra.

"How can I be serious when I just found out you love me and that you've got this sexy little lace number around your perfect breasts—"

"Quinn…"

With an exaggerated sigh, he dropped his hands and looked at her face.

"Is love enough? We've got so much to find out about each other. I mean, I don't know if I can handle it when you don't come home at nights, knowing firsthand what you go through on this job."

He smiled. "Trust me, honey, my normal days are spent in much more boring pursuits. Most of my work is via the telephone."

"But what about the days that aren't so boring?"

Quinn scooted her off his lap and walked over to his desk. When he returned, he handed her a piece of paper. "Read that."

She did. It was entitled Resignation.

"Does that answer your question?"

"No, it doesn't! Why are you quitting?"

Rolling his eyes, Quinn addressed the ceiling. "Just like a woman. She tells me she doesn't want me to be a Ranger. I tell her I'm resigning. She asks me why, like I'm crazy or something."

Kerstin gave his shin a solid kick with the toe of her shoe.

"Ouch!"

"Then stop that. And answer my question."

"I'm trading chasing criminals for chasing horses."

"Horses?"

"I told you I had horses that first day we talked

behind Daddy's Place. You know, big animals, four hooves, everyone in Texas is supposed to have one?''

She made a threatening move with her shoe and he backed away. With a feint and dash worthy of a starter for the Dallas Cowboys, he skirted her threatening foot and scooped her back onto his lap. After a moment, his mischievous smile faded, and he turned serious.

"I've finally let Haley go, Kerstin. I used the excuse that she wasn't at rest to justify my need for revenge. You healed that. I've been a peace officer for a long time, and I'm ready to move on to a new chapter in my life."

He shifted her more comfortably on his lap. "Hey, I've been wanting to tell you about something kind of spooky that happened to me a few weeks ago. Haley's brother came to see me. He said he had a dream that seemed too real not to tell me about. He said Haley told him to tell me that she's at peace and she wants me to live—really live—again. You may think that's crazy—''

"Hey, I'm a twin, remember? I don't think it's crazy at all."

He smiled. "Thanks. The long and short of it is, I think this is part of the sign that it's time for me to make some changes."

"I see," she said, not sure what else to say.

"So, will you?"

"What?"

"Marry me," he huffed impatiently, as if it had been perfectly clear.

"What if I told you I wasn't that crazy about horses?"

"Is liking horses required for an investment broker?"

"No, of course not."

"Then what does one have to do with the other? I'll have my career and you'll have yours. This is almost the new millennium, you know. Sheesh, I thought I was supposed to be the sexist one."

She gave him a warning glance, and he kissed her unrepentantly.

"I guess I just thought—"

"That I'd ask you to give up your career?"

"It sounds silly now that I'm saying it out loud. I don't know why I thought this would be an issue."

"Well, that takes care of that item. What's next?"

"What about children?"

"What about them?"

"Do you want them?" she prompted.

"Do we have to decide that now?"

"Do you know you're an exasperating man?"

"Do you know you haven't answered me?"

She fought a smile and waited until his impatience was palpable before she shrugged one shoulder.

"Well, I guess so."

He growled at her—an honest-to-pete rumble from the bottom of his throat. She laughed.

"Yes, you big lug, I'll marry you. Do you suppose

Meghan and Travis might want to have a double ceremony?''

His fingers had returned to their previous exploration of the front of her blouse. ''I'm not worried about the little details at the moment.''

She sighed in mock consternation. ''I guess we can work out the little details later, then—like where we'll live, and if we'll have children, and where we'll get married, and the rest of our lives....''

''Later sounds good to me. But for now...''

Stretching out his arm, Quinn locked his office door.

*   *   *   *   *

♥™ SILHOUETTE
DESIRE ®

AVAILABLE FROM 20TH AUGUST

A KNIGHT IN RUSTY ARMOUR Dixie Browning

Man of the Month

Coastguard Travis Holiday knew it was high time he gave up playing hero and settled down. But when he found Ruanna stranded in a storm, he decided to dust off his armour—and rescue this damsel in distress!

THE BRIDE MEANS BUSINESS Anne Marie Winston

Jillian Kerr never thought she'd see her ex-fiancé again—let alone marry him! But when the powerful executive proposed a business partnership in exchange for being his wife…she found herself saying 'I do.'

WILL AND THE HEADSTRONG FEMALE Marie Ferrarella

The Cutler Family

Sexy Will Cutler had the annoying habit of cooling Denise Cavanaugh's temper—and then heating up her hormones! But this single mum didn't have time for a man. She had a business to worry about—and a jaded heart to protect.

THIRTY-DAY FIANCÉ Leanne Banks

The Rulebreakers

Olivia Polnecek had always wanted Nick Nolan, so she was stunned when he asked her to be his fiancée for a month. She just wished she could turn their fake engagement into a real marriage!

THE RE-ENLISTED GROOM Amy J. Fetzer

Seven years ago, Maxie Parrish had left Kyle Hayden standing at the altar. Now he was back and ready to share his life with her—but he had yet to discover Maxie's precious secret…their daughter.

MIRANDA'S OUTLAW Katherine Garbera

When Miranda Colby first saw her new neighbour, he was tall, dark…and naked! The thought of spending time with Luke had innocent Miranda reeling—but could he offer her more than just short-lived passion?

Available at most branches of WH Smith, Tesco, Asda, Martins,
RS McCall, Forbuoys, Borders, Easons,
Volume One/James Thin and most good paperback bookshops

9908

AVAILABLE FROM 20TH AUGUST

Sensation

A thrilling mix of passion, adventure and drama

GABRIEL HAWK'S LADY Beverly Barton
SECONDHAND DAD Kayla Daniels
UNDERCOVER LOVER Kylie Brant
ROYAL'S CHILD Sharon Sala

Intrigue

Danger, deception and desire

NEVER LET HER GO Gayle Wilson
A FATHER FOR HER BABY B. J. Daniels
REMEMBER ME, COWBOY Caroline Burnes
TWILIGHT PHANTASIES Maggie Shayne

Special Edition

Compelling romances packed with emotion

FATHER-TO-BE Laurie Paige
THE PRESIDENT'S DAUGHTER Annette Broadrick
MEANT FOR EACH OTHER Ginna Gray
PRINCE CHARMING, M.D. Susan Mallery
BABY STARTS THE WEDDING MARCH Amy Frazier
UNTIL YOU Janis Reams Hudson

▼™ SILHOUETTE®

36 Hours

When disaster turns to passion

A THRILLING NEW 12 BOOK SERIES.

A town fights its way back from disaster…
Passions run high…
Danger is a heartbeat away…

The rainstorms and mud slides appear from
nowhere in the little Colorado town of
Grand Springs, as does the 36 hour blackout
that follows. The natural disaster causes all kinds
of chaos—the mayor dies—but it may not have been
an accident, a baby is born and abandoned and a bride races
away from the altar with a band of killers on her trail.
But sometimes, even the most life threatening situations can
inspire the most passionate romance…

Look out next month for the exciting conclusion!

Book 12 - You Must Remember This
by Marilyn Pappano
On sale 20 August

*Available at most branches of WH Smith, Tesco, Asda,
Martins, Borders, Easons, Volume One/James Thin
and all good paperback bookshops*

FREE!

4 Books
and a surprise gift!

We would like to take this opportunity to thank you for reading this Silhouette® book by offering you the chance to take FOUR more specially selected titles from the Desire™ series absolutely FREE! We're also making this offer to introduce you to the benefits of the Reader Service™—

★ FREE home delivery
★ FREE gifts and competitions
★ FREE monthly Newsletter
★ Books available before they're in the shops
★ Exclusive Reader Service discounts

Accepting these FREE books and gift places you under no obligation to buy; you may cancel at any time, even after receiving your free shipment. Simply complete your details below and return the entire page to the address below. **You don't even need a stamp!**

YES! Please send me 4 free Desire books and a surprise gift. I understand that unless you hear from me, I will receive 6 superb new titles every month for just £2.70 each, postage and packing free. I am under no obligation to purchase any books and may cancel my subscription at any time. The free books and gift will be mine to keep in any case.

D9EB

Ms/Mrs/Miss/Mr ....Initials ....
BLOCK CAPITALS PLEASE

Surname ....

Address..

....

....Postcode ....

Send this whole page to:
THE READER SERVICE, FREEPOST CN81, CROYDON, CR9 3WZ
(Eire readers please send coupon to: P.O. Box 4546, KILCOCK, COUNTY KILDARE)

Offer not valid to current Reader Service subscribers to this series. We reserve the right to refuse an application and applicants must be aged 18 years or over. Only one application per household. Terms and prices subject to change without notice. Offer expires 29th February 2000. As a result of this application, you may receive further offers from Harlequin Mills and Boon and other carefully selected companies. If you would prefer not to share in this opportunity please write to The Data Manager at the address above.

Silhouette is a registered trademark used under license.
Desire is being used as a trademark.

If you enjoyed 36 Hours,
you'll love our new 12 book series:

MONTANA

...where passions run deep and mystery lingers

Passion and romance...

Murder and mystery...

Secrets and scandals...

The mystery begins with:

Book 1 - Rogue Stallion by Diana Palmer

Special Offer

BOOK 1 FREE with selected Silhouette® series
books and book 12 of 36 Hours.

On sale 20th August 1999

*Available at most branches of WH Smith, Tesco, Asda,
Martins, Borders, Easons, Volume One / James Thin
and most good paperback bookshops*